A Moment of Comfort

Delia turned her head away, onto the viscount's chest. Lord Tyverne was there, and he was strong and real and smelled of soap, not the flowers they brought in to cover the sickroom odors. She could borrow his strength, his courage, just for a little while. He was a solider, so surely he could comprehend the need to share one's grief with someone else who understood.

Stunned, Ty could only react, not by fleeing, as he could have ordinarily done from a weeping woman, but by wrapping his arms around Miss Croft. Delia. He stroked her back. Nothing in Ty's nine and twenty years had ever felt as right as holding this woman while she cried.

Ty felt complete—that was it. Delia filled his arms perfectly, and fit precisely under his chin, her soft curves brushing against his chest. . . .

A Debt to Delia

Barbara Metzger

A SIGNET BOOK

SIGNET
Published by New American Library, a division of
Penguin Putnam Inc., 375 Hudson Street,
New York, New York 10014, U.S.A.
Penguin Books Ltd, 80 Strand,
London WC2R 0RL, England
Penguin Books Australia Ltd, Ringwood,
Victoria, Australia
Penguin Books Canada Ltd, 10 Alcorn Avenue,
Toronto, Ontario, Canada M4V 3B2
Penguin Books (N.Z.) Ltd, 182–190 Wairau Road,
Auckland 10, New Zealand

Penguin Books Ltd, Registered Offices:
Harmondsworth, Middlesex, England

First published by Signet, an imprint of New American Library,
a division of Penguin Putnam Inc.

First Printing, May 2002
10 9 8 7 6 5 4 3 2 1

Not a debt, but a dedication:
to Edith, Lady Layton,
whose heart is as big as . . . her dog.

Chapter 1

*H*e was a dead man, or as near as made no difference. His horse was already gone, put out of its misery, mercifully, with the major's last pistol shot. The officer could undoubtedly have found more ammunition somewhere on this blood-soaked, benighted field that was full of his fallen comrades, but his good right arm was shaking too badly to reload. He still had his saber, but if he took his sword hand off his slashed left shoulder, he'd likely bleed to death. No, a quick glimpse told him, he'd definitely bleed to death.

Bad enough that he was unhorsed, nearly unarmed, and dripping his life onto a scrap of foreign soil no one cared about but the natives. Worse, his uniform was still clean except for the spreading bloodstain, a scarlet beacon to any Frenchman peering through the churned-up dust. Worst still, Major Lord Tyverne—Ty to his friends, of which there were many, and his family, of which there were few—had foolishly gone and gotten himself cut down behind enemy lines. He decided to say his prayers.

Swaying on his feet, Ty first had to decide what to pray for: a quick death, forgiveness for his sins, or the chance to take at least one blasted Frog with him to the hereafter in payment for this bloody carnage.

Then he had to wonder if the Almighty was listening to prayers at all on this hell-spawned day. Looking around, he had to doubt it. He noted a large cloud of dust moving to his left, and a smaller, faster one to his right. Cavalry. This was it, then. Ty tried to convince himself that he was lucky. A lot of soldiers never made their twenty-ninth years. Half the brave lads under his command had been mere boys, just starting to shave, before they'd been hit with the French cannon.

Not for an instant did Major Tyverne consider lying beside his fallen horse, pretending to be dead. What for? He'd die soon enough anyway without a surgeon's help. Surrender? Never. Better to go down fighting now, rather than waste away in a wretched French prisoner-of-war camp, hoping for a ransom that his father would never pay.

Lud, he swore to himself, he would not go to his Maker with thoughts of that dastard the last ones on his mind. Instead, he tried to picture his beautiful mother before she passed on, his little brothers and sister, green fields, flowers, his first pony.

That was no pony thundering down on him from the right. It was a huge white charger, sweat-slicked and frothing, with a sword-wielding soldier on its back . . . a red-haired, red-coated British solider.

The man pulled up, his horse rearing on its hind legs, then leaped out of the saddle not a foot away from Ty.

"A bit of a pother, what?" he asked, assessing the major's wound and the other cloud of dust.

Ty could only nod at the rider, a lieutenant, he could see, while the younger man planted his saber in the dirt and fished in his saddlebag for a thin length of leather. He tied the thong tightly around Ty's upper arm.

"That ought to hold the bleeding until the sawbones can stitch it. Now come on aboard with you." Struggling, the slim lieutenant dragged Ty over to the horse, which was pawing at the ground and sidling away from the scent of blood.

"Dammit, Diablo, don't go getting plaguey on me now," the lieutenant ordered, heaving Tyverne into the saddle with a curse and a groan. "This is a friend, do you hear? Now take him on home, boy." He wrapped the reins around the major's right hand.

Realizing what the other man intended, Ty protested. "No, you have to come, too. We can ride double."

The lieutenant shook his red head. "Old Diablo's too tired to carry both of us that far. You're no lightweight, Major." Ty was tall, and broad, at least two stones heavier than the slight lieutenant. "We'd never make it."

"But I cannot take your horse, man!"

"Of course you can, Major. I have my pistol, my sword, and all my wits about me. I mean to make the Frenchies pay for this day's work. Now go." He lifted his hand to slap the horse's rump.

"Wait! I don't even know your name, or where to bring the horse!"

The lieutenant laughed. "Everyone knows where to bring Diablo, Major, and I will whistle for him when I get back. It's an old circus trick. Meanwhile, I am Croft, Lieutenant George Croft, at your service. I'd make a proper salute, but I doubt there's time." He brought his hand down, sending the horse forward. "Home, Diablo, take him home!"

Hanging on with his legs, since the horse seemed to need no guidance from the reins, Ty called back, "By God, I am in your debt. I owe you my life!"

The younger man laughed again, showing white teeth with a noticeable gap between the front ones. "Then fight. Live to pass on the favor. Save someone else's life."

He fought.

Ty fought the butchers to save his arm when they would have cut it off. Then he fought the infection that followed the surgeons' hasty, clumsy sewing. He struggled against taking the laudanum that would have kept him in thrall for his lifetime, and then he had to fight both the onset of the pain and the absence of the drug. He wrestled the fevers that spread throughout the army encampment, even after he'd been moved to a farmhouse and away from the disease-ridden hospital.

He fought despair, too, that his arm would never work

properly, that his career was over, that he'd lost so many fine soldiers and friends.

And then Major Lord Tyverne had to fight back his grief when they brought him Lieutenant Croft's belongings. He lost that battle, tears of guilt and anguish and remorse finally trailing down his now-gaunt cheeks, to Ty's humiliation and the mortification of Croft's chums.

One of them tried to make light of the situation as he placed a pair of worn saddlebags on the chair beside Tyverne's bed. "Old George always said that whoever could ride Diablo after he was gone could have the brute. None of us are even willing to try, so we figure that means you own the orneriest horse in the king's army, and his tack." The man, Lieutenant Harper, gestured toward the leather packs.

Ty used the sleeve of his nightshirt to brush away the signs of his weakness, pretending to be smoothing back a lock of blond hair that had fallen on his forehead. He cleared his throat. "Is . . . is the horse all right? He saved my life, you know." The horse did, and Lieutenant Croft.

"All right? Seems he was abused before George rescued him from a traveling circus or something. Now he's meaner'n ever, terrorizing the handlers and the other horses alike. That bone-crusher'd be stew for the camp followers if it weren't for your name, but we've got him penned out by himself now, waiting on you."

The men wouldn't look at the weak, fever-ridden major or his arm in its sling—wondering, Ty knew, if he'd ever be able to manage a hack, much less a highbred hell-raiser. He wondered himself, but he thanked the lieutenant's friends for their efforts.

"You won't be thanking us or old George when you try to ride him," Harper said on the way out. "No one ever did, but George and you. The grooms will be grateful when you take Diablo on home with you. They're likely praying loudest for your quick recovery."

The lieutenant's commanding officer visited the major's sickbed, too, at Ty's request. Captain Nayland had sent Croft's dress sword and trunk to the family in

Hillsdale-at-Hythe, in Kent, he reported, so yes, he could write the address for Ty. "I think there's a sister," he said with a shrug. "And a small holding, perhaps a baronetcy." After twelve years in the army, Nayland had seen too many green lieutenants come and go to give any one of them much shrift. He slept better at night, not knowing the personal details of his men, and advised Major Tyverne to do the same. "Forget Croft. He was just another soldier, doing his duty like the rest of us."

Still, the major persisted. "But was he a good officer?"

Nayland tossed aside the cigar he'd been smoking. "Good? George Croft was rash, brash, and reckless, like all the other hey-go-mad heroes who think they'll live forever. He wasn't even supposed to be in your sector that day. He had no training, no understanding of military tactics, and no fear."

In other words, Ty told himself when the other man had left, George Croft was young. The lieutenant was barely twenty, according to Nayland, nearly a decade younger than Ty himself. A landowner, a titled gentleman, he would have had his whole life ahead of him—if he hadn't sacrificed that promising future for Tyverne.

The weight of that sacrifice almost buried the major. No one since his mother had ever given him as much as a handkerchief, yet a perfect stranger had given his life. Damn, how could he pay back so great a debt to a dead man? No, he was not weeping again, not a four-year veteran of the war, not a brave leader of men with commendations from the general himself to prove it. Not Archimedes St. Ives, Viscount Tyverne, the future Earl of Stivern. The captain's rank cigar smoke was making Ty's eyes water, that was all.

For two days the lieutenant's saddlebags sat on the chair near Ty's bed before he could look inside. For two days the things perched there like a vulture, or like a judge, handing down a sentence.

The major's own friends came by when they could, bringing news of the battles, gossip from the officers' quarters, jokes from the camp, a basket of oranges from heaven knew where. They were sitting on his bed, tossing the peels on the floor and laughing when Andrew McDougall recalled a message about Tyverne's horse.

"Your new horse," he said. "The hulking gray"— which was what a white horse was called—"the one that chews boots for breakfast. The horse master sergeant says he'll keep the beast another sennight, no longer. Then it's the knackers."

So Ty had to regain his strength, and his will, for the sake of a bad-mannered brute of a horse. First he had to go through George Croft's things.

A small leather pouch held a few coins, Portugese and British. Those, and a great many more, would go to the grooms and handlers to replace and repair their ripped uniforms and shredded hats. The worn deck of cards pleased the farmer in whose bed Ty was sleeping, and the lawn handkerchiefs delighted his wife. The small pistol wrenched at Ty's gut—what if Croft had had one more weapon with him?—until he realized the weapon was jammed and would never fire again.

He sniffed at the paper-wrapped cigars and nodded. For all his bluster and sworn disinterest, Captain Nayland must have shared his tobacco with the junior officers. Ty sent them back to the captain. He tossed out some leather scraps, an unmatched glove, a broken spur, and set aside a dented flask and a bone-handled knife, sighing in relief. No treasured timepieces remained at the bottom of the bags, no miniatures of loved ones, no heirloom signet rings or family crest seals to add to Ty's burden of guilt. Just a packet of letters . . .

Chapter 2

W as it wrong to read a dead man's correspondence?
Lord Tyverne considered himself a moral man.
He had, in fact, patterned his life on precepts of honor
and duty. He would no more think of riffling through
another's personal belongings than he would consider
stealing another man's horse.

Well, the horse and the belongings, it seemed, now
belonged to him. Besides, a soldier should know better
than to leave behind anything incriminating or embarrassing, for just such eventualities. There was nothing in
Ty's own baggage, for example, that his batman could
not handle as he packed the major's trunk for the journey home. Of course, Lieutenant George Croft had not
been in the army very long, less than six months, it
seemed, so perhaps he had not thought of who would
read his diary, if he kept one, or *billets doux*, if he re-
ceived them. Yet, if Ty did not read the letters, how
could he determine if someone had more right to the
lieutenant's trappings?

The first scrap of paper was a gambling debt, scrawled
with Croft's initials, made out to one of the young officers who'd brought the saddlebags. Harper had been
decent enough not to claim the pouch of coins or the
pistol, nor to mention the debt to Tyverne. But Ty could
pay it, and would, with pleasure. The amount was minor
to him, but might mean a better meal or a decent bottle

of wine to the lieutenant. At the least, the young man
could lose it to another friend for an evening's wagering.
The junior officers had little enough to keep them occu-
pied between engagements, and card playing kept them
away from the less salubrious pastimes available to an
army encampment.

The pittance would not begin to repay the debt Ty felt
he owed, but it was a start. He set the voucher aside.

The following paper was a bill for new boots and a
hat. Diablo, it seemed, took exception to even his owner's apparel. Ty would pay that reckoning also, letting it
be known that he would honor any legitimate claim from
local merchant or army outfitter. George Croft would
not be remembered as a dirty-dish debtor.

Next on the small stack of correspondence was a letter
so creased and stained, so close to falling apart that only
spatters of candle connected the much-folded squares.
The script was nearly illegible to start with, but the water
spots and the lines crossed and recrossed, made even the
salutation and the closing indecipherable. Ty put that
page in a different pile.

Some newspaper clippings were folded together: ad-
vertisements for farm equipment, a review of a book on
sheep diseases, a yellowed gossip column mentioning a
Mrs. Clarence Croft's yellow gown, race results from
the Downs.

This was not right. Ty was feeling like a voyeur, a
trespasser. He almost gave up the job, thinking he'd send
the whole batch to the sister in Kent for her to dispose
of. The next page, however, caught his eye. A letter of
resignation, it was written in the same hand as the gaming chit, and was addressed to Croft's commanding officer. Unsent and unsigned, the thing was still disturbing.
Croft hadn't found military life to his liking? For certain
the lad was no coward. But had he begun to realize the
drudgery and futility of the army, or had he merely
been homesick?

Ty recalled his own early months in the cavalry. Older
than Croft, he'd already attained his majority—and the

all-important inheritance from his mother that permitted him to purchase his commission. One week after his birthday, he placed a wreath on her grave site, visited his two younger brothers, sent his married sister a letter, and was gone. Far from missing England, he reveled in the freedom, in being out from under his father's thumb. No general was as autocratic, no orders as arbitrary, no disapproval as harsh as the earl's. The army, with its camaraderie, its sense of order, its moral purpose of defeating the Corsican and defending the Empire, suited Viscount Tyverne to a cow's thumb.

Perhaps Croft had more to miss in his home in Kent. The letter from Croft's sister seemed to prove that.

> *My dear brother,*
> *I hope this finds you well. Actually, I hope it finds you at all, since my previous mailings must have gone astray, else you would have replied by now. Nay, you would have* <u>*appeared*</u> *by now.*

Ty leaned back against his pillows to read the rest of the letter. The script was a neat copperplate, but written small, to save the expense of posting another sheet. Miss Croft, it seemed, was of a thrifty nature, but had a great deal to say.

> *Surely you received some of my earlier postings. I regret to tell you that the Situation is more Dire than I first reported.*

Ty decided that Miss Croft was also of a dramatic bent, judging from her writing style.

> *Now I am being Shunned in the village, and even Cousin Clarence and his* <u>*dear*</u>—that emphasis gave the lie to Miss Croft's written words—*wife Gwen refuse to cross our doorstep, not even for Cook's raspberry tarts, and you know how Clarence always*

*ate more than his fair share of them, then filled his
pockets when he thought no one was looking.*
    I digress.

She certainly did. Ty wanted to know what her difficulty was, that she encouraged a soldier to sell out in the
middle of a campaign, not how gluttonous their cousin
was.

    *Clarence, through written communication, has re-
fused to release further funds. How could you have
left that pastry-stealing nodcock in charge of our
finances?*

A man who stole tarts? Ty found himself chuckling.
How indeed?

    *So we do not have the wherewithal to leave the
neighborhood where matters are so Uncomfortable.*

What, Croft's sister was being snubbed by the local
matrons for some social gaffe, so she wished to move
away from home? For that the woman thought the lieutenant should leave his post, abandon his men? Ty shook
his head, his smile fading.

    *Lord Dallsworth has let it be known, through the
vicar, who directed last Sunday's sermon directly to
our pew, I'll have you know, to my utmost mortification, that he is withdrawing his offer of marriage.*

Ty stopped smiling altogether. A gentleman did not
break off an engagement without good reason. Damn,
what bumble broth had the female embroiled herself in,
that she needed money and her brother to fix—or a
change of venue?

    *I thought of asking Aunt Rosalie in London if we
could visit with her, but she refused, saying I would*

*be welcome after this Minor Embarrassment faded
away. As if an infant is a Minor Anything. Or if it
will wash away, like a spot.*

Hell and damnation, Ty feared he understood all too
well the nature of Miss Croft's mingle-mangle, although
what the deuce she expected poor George to do about
it was a mystery to him. Carry her off to some cottage
in Wales where she could remain anonymous, he supposed. But no, the woman's next lines refuted that
possibility.

*I fear travel is no longer an option. The calcula-
tions appear to have been in error, and Time is even
shorter than Belinda and I originally believed.*

Belinda must be her maid or some such.

*I do not wish to worry you, dearest, but I am
dreadfully concerned over the eventual outcome.*

As well she should be. Not only couldn't the woman
keep her skirts down but, it seemed, she could not
even count.

What am I to do, George?

What was George to do, from the Peninsula? Lud, Ty
thought the wench must expect George to marry her off
to one of his chums, or perhaps bring the father to book.
That was just what the poor lieutenant needed, to go
home to fight a duel for his sister's honor. Better he died
here, for a worthier cause.

Ty could barely finish the letter, for his disgust, especially when the female tried to lay part of the blame on
Croft, for joining the army when he was so badly needed
at home. Well, the Crown needed good men here, too,
to keep Bonaparte from taking over the world, and so
Ty would tell the woman. In fact, he had a good mind

to tell the whining, carping Miss Croft that her letter had sent George off in a desperate frenzy, dying for an unknown officer. Women, faugh. Ty'd always believed they were the death of a man. Now he was proved right.

Your loving, anxious sister, indeed! Light-skirted executioner, more like.

George, it seemed, did not share Tyverne's outrage.

My dearest sister, Croft's unfinished letter, the last in the pile, began. No recriminations, no remonstrations. Ty supposed he was as fond of his own sister as the next man, but if she'd blotted her copybook so blatantly, he thought he might have a censorious word or two. Or three, like "How could you?" The viscount shook his head. Better make that four words; "How could you, dammit?"

Instead George asked his sister's forgiveness for not being there at her time of need. Either the man was a saint or—Ty sat up so quickly the other papers around him scattered and his injured arm protested so vehemently he fell back against the pillows until the pain subsided. He clutched the letter and stared at the whitewashed ceiling above him. Lord, what if the poor girl had been violated? He knew small towns and small minds would not make the distinction between wanton and raped. Ruined was ruined, and no so-called decent folk would come to her aid. Of course she'd want to move, to pass herself off as a widow somewhere, after her own family, the cousins, the aunt in London, had turned their backs on her. Without money or friends, heaven alone knew what would happen to Miss Croft. Without George . . . It did not bear thinking of. His letter continued:

> *I swear I would never have left you to bear this on your own, if only I had known in time.*

Ty's brows were drawn into a scowl as he read further.

> *And I will write to Clarence this very day to release to you whatever funds you need, even if he has to*

mortgage Faircroft. Hire the best physicians, or send to London for one of those fancy accoucheurs if you think that would be better. Do what you must, Dilly girl—

Dilly? What kind of name was Dilly? Ty looked back, but Miss Croft had not given her name, only Sister.

—until I can get home.

Major Tyverne clenched his jaw muscles. Croft had been intending to go to his sister's aid, for whatever good he could do.

I did ask the captain for leave as soon as I got your last letter, and Belinda's, of course, but he refused, with a major battle looming. I swear I shall make sure I am wounded in the skirmish—nothing serious, mind you, so do not fret over me when you have so much else in your dish—but enough that they will have to send me home.

Ty's teeth would be ground to nubs at this rate.

If not, I shall resign my commission, enduring the label of coward, as you at home have endured worse.

Ty could well imagine the taunts an unwed, enceinte miss would hear, the whispered slurs she would not. The turned backs, the disrespect—How could a gently reared female bear that on her own? Now to add the grief of George's passing was beyond cruel.

Lud knew what would happen to her or the child without Croft's support. That cousin, Clarence, sounded just the kind of toad to toss them out on the street. If George's sister gave up the babe, as many a woman in her circumstances would be forced to, she would still never be welcomed in the community, never given references for employment, never have the chance to marry.

Not even jingle-brained George, who thought he could orchestrate the depth and degree of a battle wound, believed his sister could find a husband.

As for Lord Dallsworth, I cannot regret the termination of his suit. You never wished to accept that old stick anyway, you know. You told me often enough. Furthermore, I refuse to have a sister known as Dilly Dally.

George closed his letter by beseeching his sibling to be strong, for all of them. He promised to finish the letter after the coming battle, when he could better estimate his arrival date.

The lieutenant never finished the letter, of course, and he was never going to arrive in Kent. Not in time for the baby, not in time to rescue his sister. Never.

"Live," he'd told Ty. "Live to pass on the favor. Save someone else's life."

Major Lord Tyverne always paid his debts. With one notable exception, he always fulfilled his obligations. He knew what he had to do now.

He had to ride the blasted horse.

Chapter 3

A nearly useless arm was bad enough. Fevers that kept racking his weakened body were worse. Landing on his rump in front of half the regiment was worst of all.

The surgeons had declared Major Lord Tyverne recovered enough so that the ride home in the troop transport ship would not kill him. They would certainly make no such assurances about riding, much less mounting a half-wild, man-hating gelding. So Ty did not tell them.

The horse did not seem to recall that George had labeled Tyverne a friend, despite Ty's repeated avowals as he dodged flying hooves and slashing teeth. Diablo did not like boots with tassels, boots with fold-over white tops. He did not like loose ends on neck cloths, fluttering handkerchiefs, or gloves. He detested spurs, crops, ropes, or chains. He liked hats. A good hat could keep the wretch entertained for hours, running from the irate owner, stomping on it, shredding it. The more expensive the headpiece, the more enjoyment Diablo seemed to derive.

What he really loved, however, was boiled rum balls. He'd take a peppermint drop if nothing better was offered, sugared almonds or a biscuit on occasion, washed down with a pailful of ale, but the big gelding really savored rum balls. He'd roll the hard candy around in his mouth, his eyes closed, white velvet nostrils whuffling in contentment. He'd let Ty mount then, without attacking the buttons or braid on his uniform. When the candy was gone, though, and the gelding noticed the heavier than usual weight on his back . . .

Everyone said it was a miracle the major didn't break his fool head, and a greater miracle he didn't shoot the fool horse. Soon enough the gelding realized Ty wasn't giving up, and wasn't running out of rum balls. The horse and his new owner came to terms, luckily before Ty came to grief or reopened his wounded arm. Every cook and camp follower with a cauldron made a fortune, making candy, and Ty made arrangements to sail home, praying he'd be in time.

Delia Croft had almost no time to herself anymore, but she stole a few precious minutes that afternoon to walk from Faircroft House to the high road. She needed to escape the grief and desperation inside, where Aunt Eliza was constantly weeping and Nanny was praying, and Belinda was lost in her own pain. Delia feared she'd go mad inside, with nothing but sorrow for company. She was searching the garden path for daffodil tips, snow-drops, birds singing courting songs, buds on the trees, anything to show that spring was truly coming, that this endless winter might be over at last, that life went on. In truth, she was seeking solutions to questions with no answers.

What was she to do? Delia was running out of choices, money, and hope. No one was going to come to her aid now, for even distant relations and casual friends had heard of the family's disgrace and turned deaf ears to her pleas. Even condolences for poor George were perfunctory at best, grudgingly given. No one wished to share her burdens.

Delia fingered the ugly, uneven black of her gown, thinking of what mourning rituals she'd had to forego. She'd had to dye her old dresses rather than spend the money for new gowns. What blunt she did have—her own funds, which Cousin Clarence could not deny her—were going for doctors and medicines and additional servants to help in the house, which clutch-fisted Clarence could, and did, refuse to finance.

She could support herself, Delia had calculated, in a modest manner, but never the others. She could seek employment, for she was strong and healthy, one-and-twenty, and reasonably educated. Delia thought she'd make a decent companion for an older woman, if she could find anyone willing to give her references. Without them, she could throw herself on her aunt Rosalie's mercy in London, being an unpaid companion, she supposed, instead of a paid employee. She most likely could even stay on here, when Clarence and Gwen moved into Faircroft House, as an unpaid housekeeper. But not the others. Clarence's wife would never permit the others to live at Faircroft.

Eliza Linbury was Delia's mother's spinster sister, with no claims on the Croft side of the family. Nanny had been nursemaid to the Linbury girls, and was far too old to take on a new family of youngsters, especially Gwen's unruly, undisciplined brood. Besides, Gwen already had her own woman to care for the unattractive, unappealing trio, thank goodness.

As for Belinda, she was no relation to the Crofts whatsoever, and Clarence refused to accept responsibility for her at all. Gwen refused to speak her name out loud. Delia, however, could no more throw Miss Gannon out of the house than she could Nanny or Aunt Eliza, for as long as she had the house. She supposed she ought to be thankful to Clarence and Gwen for letting them stay on until the baby arrived. Theirs was stone-cold charity, however, refusing to enter their new inheritance while it was under such a cloud.

After the birth? Delia could not imagine what was to become of them. Without George, she had almost no options left. She was a mere woman, without income, without a profession. Heavens, she no longer had a home to call her own. Marriage was a wisp of a possibility, since she still had her dowry—or Clarence did—if Aunt

Rosalie could find a gentleman willing to marry a tarnished bride, with such encumbrances. No, Delia thought, any man so willing would merely want a bed warmer, a brood mare, an unpaid bondwoman. Miss Croft would rather be paid for her labor, she decided, and she'd rather clean chimneys than cater to any such man. If she married, a rapidly fading dream, she'd wed for love or not at all. Hadn't she turned down Lord Dallsworth numerous times? She could have had security, a home, a settled future—at the cost of sharing them with Lord Dallsworth. She shuddered, and not from the cold seeping through her cloak. Not for a minute did she regret refusing the baron when George was alive to support her and her decision. Dallsworth would not have supported her dependents now.

For the millionth time, Delia wondered how George could have left them like this, how they were to go on. The daffodils would bloom, the trees would unfurl new leaves, a baby would come into the world—the ultimate miracle—and she'd have another mouth to feed.

Exhausted from worry and work, Delia sank down onto the hard bench beneath the bare-branched lilacs, glad of the solitude. Inside the house she was alone in the midst of the other women, more alone than she'd been in her life, but having to be strong for their sakes. Now, out here, she could confess to herself that she missed her mother, dead these six years, and her father, gone for two. They had always sheltered her, cared for her, guided her. She missed dear bacon-brained George, despite all his faults, the worst of which, of course, was dying.

Delia dabbed at her eyes with the mobcap she'd taken to wearing in a vain attempt to appear more respectable, as if a cap were going to prove her decency when over twenty years of virtue had not.

Foolish, foolish girl, she chided herself, tears would not pay the piper. She pulled the cap back on, over the long coiled braid she wore for simplicity these days. She tucked a few errant red locks beneath the brim, and rose from the bench. Enough of privacy and self-pity, she told herself. She had things to do, preparations to make. The baby would need clothes whether it had a father or not.

On her way back toward the house, Delia paused when she heard a horse on the high road. She waited to see if the rider passed on, although heaven knew she was not expecting company. The horse trotted to the gates to Faircroft, slowed, and turned up the drive. Delia saw the big horse, so pale as to be snowy white in the sun, and the rider in a scarlet coat.

George had come home after all! The army was wrong, they'd buried the wrong man! "Mindle," she shouted toward the house and her waiting butler, her father's old valet, "Mindle, get Aunt Lizzie, get everyone. Come see who has—"

It was not George, of course.

The bare-headed rider had fair hair, Delia could see now, not George's flame-shaded red. He was bigger, bulkier than her slim brother, and he had a deal more gold trim and ribbons on his regimental jacket. Most telling of all, he sat like a sack in the saddle. George would never have slouched that way, nor would he have held Diablo on such a loose rein, not that horse, not if he wished to arrive home intact.

Horse and rider made a weaving course up the garden path, trampling one of the budding primroses along the way.

Heavens, Delia thought, the man was foxed! She was glad she'd called for Mindle, for they'd all heard frightening stories of returning soldiers turning to crime. Dover, the new boy she'd recently hired, also came from around the side of the house at her shout, a water bucket in his hand. Her allies might be barely seven and pushing seventy, but they were better than nothing.

Ty knew it was a miracle he hadn't fallen out of the saddle long since. If the horse had not seemed to know the way, they'd never have arrived. As it was, every step Diablo took drove spikes of pain through his head. His hands were trembling, and he could barely see the ground ahead. But he was close, and he was going to pay his debt to George Croft if it killed him.

Thank God he did not have to call out to the house, for his lips were parched and his tongue was thick, and he'd been clenching his teeth so tightly against the pain that he doubted he could have opened his mouth. A woman was waiting for him, though. The right woman. Unless he was hallucinating again, George Croft's sister was waiting for him, in some mysterious way he'd have to think about later. That had to be she, standing in front of the door like a vixen defending her den. A red curl trailed down the shoulder of her mourning gown. She seemed to have Croft's same slender build. No, that could not be right, unless he was too late. He could not be too late. He *would* not be too late.

"M-m'Crof?" Ty croaked as the horse came to a halt a few feet from the woman.

She nodded.

He dismounted. What he actually did was take his feet out of the stirrups, swing one leg over, and slide, holding onto the saddle with his good hand, praying Diablo would not pick now to get up to his old tricks.

No one moved. Even in his fevered state, Ty's soldier's instincts told him two men were approaching from an outbuilding, one with a pitchfork, and two others were taking positions at Miss Croft's sides. Zeus, they must think him a footpad.

He tried a bow, with one hand still on Diablo's saddle for balance. "Ty. T-tyverne," he mumbled.

"No, this is not a tavern," Miss Croft stated. "There is an inn in the village. Now, get back on your horse and leave us be."

The man with the pitchfork waved it, in threat. Diablo hopped away, ears laid back, nostrils flaring.

Left with no support, Ty took a wavering step forward. Miss Croft's minions closed ranks. The elderly servant brandished a silver teapot and polishing cloth. The boy raised a heavy wooden bucket.

"No harm," Ty managed to say. "George Croft . . . a debt."

Miss Croft did not unbend an iota. "Whatever was between you and George shall have to stay that way. I refuse to be held responsible for George's gaming debts, on top of everything else."

"Not . . . a game. My life." Tyverne had to bite back a moan as he stumbled one step closer. He raised his arms to prove he came in peace, which was a fatal mistake for his precarious balance. Falling to his knees, just before he fell unconscious, the viscount finally delivered his message: "And I have come to marry you."

Chapter 4

$\mathcal{A}$ s far as proposals went, this one went beyond the pale, which just went to prove that when things were at their most dismal, they could always get worse.

Fusty old Lord Dallsworth had made Delia three awkward and embarrassing offers in form, but he never made a May game of her in front of half her staff. Nor had he required courage from a bottle to tender his troth.

This man, this absolute and absurd stranger, was undeniably foxed. Why, he positively reeked of spirits. So did his horse. The horse, incidentally, having frightened off the gardener and Jed Groom, seemed about to stomp the jug-bitten soldier to death, nuzzling at his pockets, while Delia gave a fair imitation of Lot's wife. She managed to rouse herself from her horrified paralysis enough to shove the horse away from the still-lying sot, which cost her the ugly mobcap, and a few long red hairs with it.

Rubbing her head, Delia watched the horse prance off with his booty. That was George's mount, all right, the devil's own namesake, that had taken them ages to tame after rescuing him from the circus. The only good thing about George going off to war was that he'd taken the troublesome trooper with him. Now Diablo was back, with a drunk on his back.

Well, neither horse nor high-seas-over soldier was staying. Delia reached for the bucket her newest servant held. If Dover's pail contained water, fine. If slops, too bad for the big, handsome fellow and his clean uniform. She was about to toss the contents over the unconscious officer when she noticed his arm shaking. She also took time to note the high color in his cheeks and the dampness of the hair plastered to his forehead.

She gingerly reached a finger to touch the stranger's face, but swiftly drew her hand away. "Confound it, the man is sick, not inebriated," she told her waiting subordinates. "He is burning with fever. The man wasn't pot-valiant when he'd made his offer; he was delirious."

The boy backed away, but Mindle bent over, his joints creaking, to see for himself. "Dangerously ill, I would say. What shall we do with him, Miss Delia?"

"Heavens, I have no idea."

"Well, you cannot bring him in here, Dilly," Aunt Eliza called from the doorway, where she was shredding her handkerchief and dabbing at her eyes. "Heaven knows we have enough sickness and woe. And we could all come down with whatever infection he carries. What would we do then?"

"But we cannot simply leave him here either, Aunt. He quite ruins the scenery, don't you think?" she jested, trying to think. "I suppose we can haul him onto a wagon and drive him to the village."

"I doubt they'd take such a sick one at the inn," Mindle said. The old man was still bent over, searching through the stranger's pockets for his identification. He held up a heavy purse. "Despite his blunt."

"No, and he would not get much care there, if Molly Whitaker did deign to give him a bed," Delia agreed.

Aunt Eliza sniffed. "Molly Whitaker would not give clean sheets to the bishop. But the vicar could take him in, or the apothecary."

The soldier groaned and, without thinking, Delia knelt to put her hand under his head, to cushion it from the ground while they decided what to do. She wiped his forehead with her handkerchief, and sent Dover to fill his bucket with clean water.

"Dilly, keep away from him!" Aunt Eliza shrieked.

"He is diseased!" She held her handkerchief over her mouth and nose.

From another pocket, Mindle handed Delia a small brown-paper packet of medicinal powders marked "Fever" on the label. Delia sniffed at it. "I suppose this means he has some recurring illness, not a contagion. Nanny might know what the stuff is and how to give it to him. Or else Mags will." Mags was the local herb woman and midwife, who was already calling at Faircroft House on a daily basis.

"Then send him to Mags's place. She can care for him."

"In her one-room thatched cottage, with drying plants hanging everywhere?"

"That makes no never mind," Aunt Eliza declared, back to wringing her handkerchief between twitching fingers. "He cannot come in here! For all we know he is a deserter, a ruffian who will murder us all in our beds."

Mindle handed her a calling card from a silver case.

"No, Aunt," Delia said after reading the expensive vellum card, "our caller appears to be an officer. A major, not a marauder. And a gentleman. Not that they cannot be one and the same, but I do think our uninvited guest is too ill to pose much danger."

"A gentleman, you say?" Aunt Eliza came closer, peering over Delia's shoulder. "My, he is a handsome fellow, isn't he?"

He might be the most handsome man Delia had ever seen, if not for the gauntness about his cheekbones and the stubble on his jaw. The small scar over one golden eyebrow merely added distinction, and the aristocratic, slightly aquiline nose lent character to an otherwise classically molded face. She'd wager his eyes were blue, under long, thick lashes that any female would envy. She sighed.

Aunt Eliza sighed, too. "You still cannot bring him in here. If you are not going to think of the rest of us, dear, think of your reputation."

Delia brushed that aside, with the lock of hair that

had fallen across Major Lord Tyverne's forehead. Her reputation had already sunk so low, she could dance on the tabletop at Molly Whitaker's pub without shocking anyone.

"He did say that Master George saved his life," Mindle volunteered.

"An' they say as how iffen you save a bloke's life, you're s'posed to watch out for him forever," Dover put in, back with the water and a clean towel.

Delia smiled at the boy for remembering the cloth. "Clever lad, but that's just an old wives' tale." And wasn't it just like George to leave her another burden, if it were true. She dipped the cloth into the water and dribbled some onto his lordships's dry lips. "A viscount is not like some puppy you rescue from a ditch, you know. Besides, if my brother saved this man's life—"

"A viscount?" Aunt Eliza squealed. "You never said he was a viscount. Tyverne? Isn't that the St. Ives heir? Heavens, child, this man might be the next Earl of Stivern! Why, whatever are you thinking, Dilly? The dear boy could catch his death of cold out here on the ground."

Delia was thinking that she did not need one more problem on her plate, but her aunt was calling for the gardener and the stable hand to come help get their guest indoors.

Jed Groom was willing to assist with the officer. Diablo was a horse of another color.

"I'll help with the horse, Miss Delia," young Dover offered, eager to do anything for the adored mistress who'd rescued him from the workhouse.

"No!" she and Jed and the gardener all yelled at once, lest the boy get tossed around and trampled like Delia's cap.

"Diablo was mistreated in his early years," Delia explained to the crestfallen boy who thought he'd done something wrong, to be shouted at. "Now he does not like men, and Heaven knows what he'd do to a boy."

"But he let the major ride him, din't he?"

He did, which told Delia a lot about the sick man, his strength, his skill, and his sheer stubbornness. She turned to the groom and said, "Just open the stall door and put out Diablo's grain, Jed. And get Cook started soaking sugar cubes in brandy, even if we have to go without supper."

She directed the rest of her small staff—two day maids and the cook's helper—to bring a bed frame and mattress down from the attics, and turn the small, unused rear parlor into a guest room. The windows leaked there, but they would have to keep the fires lit anyway. That way they would not have to drag the large gentleman up the narrow flights, and could lend a modicum of respectability, like her lost cap, to a decidedly havey-cavey business by keeping him away from the family quarters—and Belinda. Besides, this was a temporary arrangement only, Delia prayed. Very temporary.

While Mindle and the groom got his lordship settled, and Nanny fussed over him and his medication, Delia wrote a letter to her cousin Clarence—Sir Clarence now, as his wife was quick to remind everyone. They'd hear soon enough from the servants' grapevine tonight, or the egg man in the morning. Better they learn about the major now, from Delia. Besides, if Tyverne's life had been in George's keeping, Clarence must have inherited him along with the baronetcy and the estate. Clarence and Gwen were welcome to the ailing, addlepated gentleman, with Delia's blessings. She certainly had no time for a bedlamite beau.

Not that Delia mentioned his lordship's proposal to her cousins, naturally. There was nothing in the offer worth the ink to write it. The man was raving, obviously out of his mind. Of course any man foolish enough to ride Diablo when he was in such ill health, or to make such an outrageous proposal, could not be altogether needle-witted at the best of times.

Delia did permit herself an instant's wool-gathering, a smile playing about her lips. After all, it was not every day a handsome gentleman prostrated himself at her feet.

Wasn't it every girl's dream to be rescued from peril by a handsome knight on a pure white steed? He'd carry her off to a magical realm where troubles were forbidden, where they would live happily ever after in a rosy glow of eternal love.

In a storybook.

In actual fact, the man was likely here to return Diablo. She did write of that possibility to Clarence, cheered to think of her custard-soft, corpulent cousin trying to ride George's gelding.

When the letter was sanded and sealed, she checked on his lordship, now made more comfortable in bed, in one of George's old nightshirts. She supposed the hem wouldn't reach the major's knees, and the sleeves left his wrists uncovered, but the man was sleeping soundly. Nanny assured her that, with the fever under control, her prime specimen of British manhood would be right as a trivet in a day or two, except for the scar on his upper arm. That wound might never heal properly, Nanny tsk'ed, but she'd pray for him. Delia left Nanny and her Bible at the gentleman's bedside, and made sure that Aunt Eliza kept watch over Belinda.

Then, calling for the boy Dover to accompany her, she put on her old chip-straw bonnet, which had taken the black dye even less successfully than her gowns, and told Mindle she was walking to the village to deliver her letter. Delia had to make certain, she told the old servant, that the major hadn't taken rooms at the inn, or had his valet and bags waiting somewhere. A gentleman simply did not travel with the one clean shirt they'd found in his saddlebag, once they had wrestled the saddle off the impossible horse. Perhaps the major had a wife waiting for him in the next village, she added, to put paid to any speculation on her loyal servant's part.

As an afterthought, Delia decided to take Belinda's poor dog with her. Heaven knew the fat little white terrier needed the exercise.

They stopped first at Clarence's father-in-law's house outside the village, where her cousin and his wife resided with the old squeeze-crab. A surly footman opened the door, took one look at the ragged boy, the bedraggled dog, and Miss Croft in her ratty hat, and nearly closed the door on them. No wonder Clarence and Gwen were so eager to move into their own establishment, Delia decided after she convinced the lackey to deliver her letter. The house was dark, dreary, and cold, about as welcoming as the spotty-faced, sour-breathed servant.

They visited Whitaker's Inn after that, then the vicarage, the livery, and Mrs. Hensell's, who sometimes took in travelers. No one knew of the ailing officer, or of anyone asking for him. Now, though, they all knew that Miss Delia Croft of Faircroft House was sheltering a wounded friend of her deceased brother's. It wasn't what anyone could like, of course, but what else was she to do with a gallant officer of the Peninsular Campaign? Obviously there was nothing hole-in-corner about the situation, for Miss Croft was not making the least effort to keep the matter quiet, was she?

Delia's plan was working, except for the Farthingale sisters, who pulled their skirts away from Delia's contamination in the everything store. The merchants were more friendly than they had been in weeks, though, when they saw how Miss Croft intended to increase her orders for her unfortunate guest.

Invalid food would not put meat back on a wounded man's bones, the butcher agreed, tossing a scrap to Belinda's little dog.

A highbred horse like Sir George's needed more oats and fresh bedding than Miss Croft kept on hand for her old mare. Jack Browne at the livery would load up a wagon.

Naturally the apothecary could mix more fever medicine. Mr. Clayton handed Dover a peppermint stick, without charge, while filling a large sack with lemon drops.

Soothing teas, the latest books from the lending library, the most recent London journals, a new shaving kit, a bottle of port. Whatever else Delia could think of a gentleman needing, she ordered. Oh, and she directed all the bills to her cousin, since the viscount was, of course, actually Sir Clarence's guest.

Chapter 5

*M*oaning. Weeping. Praying.

He was back at the field hospital. But Ty could not open his eyes, and the prayers were at his bedside. He must be dead then, with coins placed on his lids so he wouldn't be staring upward at eternity. Odd, though, that the Spanish nun was reciting the Bible in English, and he smelled—yes, a mustard plaster on his chest.

He jerked himself up and pulled the heavy damp cloth from over his eyes. If he was dead, they'd laid him out in a parlor, for he could see a sofa and a deal table, china figurines on a mantel. "What the devil?"

An old woman shook her finger at him. "There will be no blasphemy in Faircroft House, young man."

Not dead, then, but in Kent. It all came back to him, the storm-tossed sail home, the hurried stop in London, the mad ride to Kent, the race against time and nature. He had absolutely no idea who this woman was, nor why he was sleeping in a parlor, in a too small nightshirt. "You are . . . ?"

"Nanny, my lord. I helped raise up Master Georgie and Miss Dilly, and their mum and Miss Lizzie before them. If the Good Lord is willing, I will help swaddle the next generation."

"The baby . . . ?"

"Know about that, do you, my lord? Aye, if you are that good a friend of Master Georgie's, you would know."

Ty did not have the energy to explain that he'd known George Croft for less than five minutes. "Has it come?"

"When the Good Lord decides the time is right, He tells us."

Ty wished he were on such speaking terms with the Almighty, for he still had no idea if Miss Croft had borne her illegitimate infant. He vaguely recalled a slender young female at the entrance to the house when he'd ridden up. He'd practically fallen at her feet before he'd lost consciousness. There was something else his befogged mind was trying to remember, something she'd said, or he'd said. He'd given his name and then—"Bloody hell! I proposed to the wrong woman!"

Nanny poured a sleeping draught down his throat.

Delia returned to Faircroft in a much better frame of mind than when she had left. Just getting away from the house, getting some fresh air and exercise, and getting nods from some of her neighbors, worked wonders. Now she could even face with equanimity this new coil of George's creation, and ascertain how soon he would be ready to leave.

Mindle reported that his lordship was still sleeping, and would be for some time yet. Nanny, it seemed, had declared that sleep was most helpful for the officer's recovery, after muttering something about heathens and heretics and heroes. Delia shrugged, used to Nanny's sermons, and decided to steal a few more minutes of freedom. She would go check on the horse.

Sending young Dover inside with most of the parcels, Delia kept only the sack of sweets with her. Unaware that Belinda's little dog had followed her, and the treats, from the house, Delia held a candy out to the gelding, through the bars of the stall gate. The sweet rolled off her gloved palm, and the furry white terrier chased it, under the door, nearly under Diablo's feet.

"Oh, no," Delia said with a moan. The dog meant the world to Belinda, who had so little. She could not lose her pet, too. Delia started tossing lemon drops for Diablo

to the other side of the stall, away from the dog. The
stupid mutt started chasing them, too, yapping excitedly
at this new game instead of coming to Miss Croft's calls.

Diablo's ears were twitching, not a good sign, Delia
knew from experience. She held a peppermint stick in
her hand. "Come on, you spawn of the devil, you. Any
other horse would prefer a carrot, or an apple, but not
you. You have to have expensive candies. Well, here."

The big horse was more interested in the trespasser.
He lowered his head, with those massive grinding molars,
toward the dog.

"If you injure that animal," Delia threatened, "you'll
be pulling dung carts in Hades. You'll be ground up for
swine food and . . . and your hair will be used for stuffing
furniture. Ugly furniture, like in Gwen's father's house."

Horse and dog touched noses, and Delia let out the
breath she'd been holding. Some horses liked having a
companion in their stables: a pony, a donkey, a cat. Why
not a small dog? Because Diablo was a mean son of a
stallion, that was why.

Delia knew she couldn't scream or wave her hands.
Diablo was liable to step on the buffle-headed bitch by
mistake. She did the only thing she could think of to
distract the gelding while she slipped into the stall and
scooped up the foolhardy fur-ball: she gave Diablo her
chip-straw bonnet.

"And I hope the dye turns your teeth black, you miserable, misbegotten nag." Delia found herself weeping into
the dog's fur. "How could you come home without
George?"

Moaning. Weeping. No praying, thank God. Or not.

This time Ty knew he was alive because he hurt too
much. Perhaps the moans had come from his own dry-
as-dust mouth. Someone was prodding and poking at the
tender flesh around his wounded arm.

"Don't take it!" he shouted, coming fully alert with a
start, to find another old woman, a different one, leaning
over him. This one was dressed in brown homespun, with

a thick knitted shawl over her shoulders. She had frown lines around her mouth, and she smelled of asafetida.

"Tscha," the old crone said. "I'm merely checking the handiwork what passes for doctoring these days. I be old Mags, my lord, the healer hereabouts, and I've seen neater stitching on a five-year-old's sampler."

Ty did not look. He pulled the edges of his borrowed nightshirt together with what dignity he could, considering he was flat on his back and weak as a kitten. "At least they left me my arm, and I can use it somewhat."

"Aye, I give you that. A'course, you'll have this ugly scar for the rest of your life. I could of done better." She pulled open his collar again and slathered some foul-smelling salve on the wound. "This might help, late though it is."

Ty wrinkled his nose. "That smells like something they put on horses."

"Works, doesn't it? Might take some of the stiffness out, if you start using it more." She wiped her hands on a bit of sacking and stowed the jar in a basket at her feet. "A'course, you'll have the fevers for the rest of your life, too, I s'pose. Can't do much about that, more's the pity. Liable to come on you anytime, especially you go off half-cocked, riding cross-country in the cold."

"Yes, so the physicians warned me." Ty had not listened to them, and he did not intend to listen to an old country witch. "But now that you have done with cheering up your patient, Mistress Mags, perhaps you could give me some information. Such as Miss Croft's condition . . . ?"

Mags lowered her brow. "As good as can be expected, considering her woes. She's a good lass, is our Miss Dilly, and don't you go forgetting it."

Since the hag was even then holding his nose to make him swallow yet another noxious brew, Ty was not liable to forget.

"And the infant?" he managed to ask after drinking the barley water she held out, to rid himself of the other taste.

Mags shook her head. "That's out of my hands now."

Why would no one tell him whose hands the child *was* in? Ty could feel the drowsiness seep through him, but he had to know more. "How soon . . . ?"

"How soon can you be up and finding more ways to destroy your health that the French and the physicans haven't? A sennight or so, I'd guess, before you regain strength enough to sit in the saddle."

"No, too long. I have to be back. Promised."

"In a hurry to kill yourself, are you?"

Ty's eyes were drifting closed, despite his best efforts to stay awake. "London . . . my . . . Nonny."

Mags pursed her lips. "I don't care how many bits of muslin you have waiting for you in the City. You wouldn't be much good to her anyway, sweating and shaking. Mayhaps you could ride back in a carriage sooner. We'll see how you fare on the morrow."

Ty was already snoring softly when Mags left, telling the sleeping gentleman, "An' the sooner you're out of here and on your way the better, I'm thinking."

"He won't be a-lingering long," Mags reported to Delia before she left.

"You mean he is going to die?" Delia asked with a quick intake of air. She could not bear to think of another death. Not his lordship, not now. "How could he die, such a big, strong man? He's so young and . . . and . . ."

"Manly?" Mags snorted. "He is that, a fine broth of a fellow. No, he's not going to stick his spoon in the wall, not that I can see, anyways. But he's not the staying kind, so don't you go thinking he is, missy."

"Of course not. He is a soldier and a lord. He'd never wish to recuperate here, in some pawky back parlor."

"That's not what I meant," Mags muttered, not wanting to speak of London ladybirds, not to a young lady like Miss Croft. Of course, Miss Dilly was already seeing more of the grimmer sides of life than a gently bred female ought. "He doesn't seem high in the instep. But the man has business in the City."

"Naturally. As soon as he is well enough to give us his direction, I'll inform his people to come fetch him." She turned to go down the hall to the rear parlor, but Mags put a hand on her sleeve.

"Nay, he's sleeping. Don't disturb his rest, Miss Dilly. In fact, you ought to keep out of there altogether. Let Mindle look after him."

"But you said he was not contagious."

There were more catchy things than the influenza, Mags knew. "Just keep away from him. You don't belong in there."

"What, did he swear at you, too? Nanny gave me strict orders to stay away from his sickroom, declaring the major's language fit only for barracks and barrooms. I suppose that comes from being a soldier. I daresay I have heard as bad from the stable hands."

No, the officer had given Mags a sweet smile, in fact, despite his pain and suffering. It was that smile that worried her more than curses or contagions. "I, ah, was worrying about your reputation."

Delia had to laugh. "The man is already in my house. How could my reputation be any more tarnished by speaking to the major—and who is to tell?"

Mags fussed with her basket, sudden color in her lined cheeks.

"Why, Mags, I do believe you've heard talk and fear for my virtue, that my head will be turned by the major's handsome face!" She laughed outright. "As if I believed a word of his dunderheaded declaration. The man was out of his mind, and I'd be out of mine to believe an officer, a titled gentleman at that, could be interested in me." She held out her arms, emphasizing her too thin form, the dreary black gown, the dark smudges under her eyes. "Why, I even have freckles. No, I will speak with our guest about George, and then send him on his way as soon as he is fit. And do not worry, Mindle and

Aunt Eliza have agreed to take turns sitting up with him tonight, while Nanny and I keep watch over Belinda." The humor left her eyes. "I don't suppose there is any change."

Mags could only shake her head. "I've tried every remedy I know, and a few I can only guess at. Nothing seems to help."

"Then the sooner we are rid of George's friend, the better."

Chapter 6

*W*eeping.

Ty decided he must have died and gone to Hell after all, for his notion of Purgatory was a parlor filled with crying females.

How many old women lived in this house anyway? This one was quietly snuffling into a frivolously useless lace handkerchief at his bedside, her needlework forgotten in her lap. She had a lace cap tied under her chin, but Ty could see the long reddish braid on her shoulder, even by the soft candlelight and the glow from the fireplace. George's aunt, if he did not miss his guess.

He cleared his throat, and the woman hastily lowered the handkerchief and tried to give him a watery smile. "You're awake."

Definitely George's relation, for while Lieutenant Croft had an obvious space between his top front teeth, this woman had a gap wide enough to drive a coach through. He wondered if George's sister had the odd defect. Hell, he wondered if George's sister had an odd kick to her gallop. "Miss Croft?"

"Oh, no. I am Miss Linbury, on George's mother's side, you know. No, you wouldn't, would you? I am Miss Eliza Linbury, but you can call me Aunt Eliza. Or Aunt Lizzie. Everyone does. Not the servants, of course, which would be disrespectful, but you are not. A servant, I mean, although I am certain you would not be disrespectful, either. Of course I suppose I have no way of knowing, since some young gentlemen do not have the proper regard for their elders, or—Where was I?"

Tending the pigeons that were roosting in her cockloft, if Ty had to guess. She did not wait for an answer, luckily, or he would be hard-pressed, indeed, to show the proper regard.

"Oh, yes, I recall. I was telling you to call me Aunt Lizzie if you are to become part of the—that is, if you are going to—Oh, dear." She began to whimper again, and to twist the handkerchief between her hands.

"Miss Eliza will do for now, ma'am, don't you think?" Ty quickly told her. He was exhausted already, without another sleeping potion. "And I am Tyverne."

"Of course you are, dear boy. I would not be quite so in alt if you were not. La, I mean to say I would not be so pleased if you could not recall your name. Fevers do that to a body occasionally, you know." She briefly smiled again, then fluttered her handkerchief in the direction of a china tea set on a nearby table. "I was just about to have a dish of tea. Will you join me?"

Ty nodded. He'd give anything for a cup of tea, not barley water or the broth they'd been spooning down him. Actually he'd like a beefsteak, but the poppy seed cake he spied would do for now.

"Cream? Sugar?"

"Both, please."

"Good, that's just the way I like my tea."

She added twice more of both than he wished and then, to Ty's dismay, tucked a serviette under his chin. At least Miss Linbury was not intending to feed him, he was relieved to see as she took up her own cup and saucer. Once she had taken a sip, though, she asked, "Yes, but is that Viscount Tyverne or Major Tyverne? I mean, should we address you as major since you were in uniform, or my lord, since you are not now? Of course, you were a viscount before you were an officer, and will be after, one would hope. On the other hand, yours is an honorary title, while your army ranking—"

Ty was not certain what the future would bring. The

War Office would gladly keep him on in London as an administrative officer or a liaison, but the army Ty belonged with was the one in the field, with his men. He was no longer fit for that life. Lud only knew if he were fit for civilian life, but he did have responsibilities to his family. To this family, too. "I am not sure about selling out yet," he replied while Miss Croft was in mid-blather. "But I think I would prefer Tyverne or Ty to either rank or title."

Miss Linbury daintily patted her lips. "I shall call you Tyverne, then, until you become— That is, are you married?"

He almost spilled the tea down the front of the night-shirt. "Lud, no."

She beamed at him—Ty thought he could see her tonsils through the space in her teeth—and held out the platter of cake slices.

Ty choked on a mouthful of poppy seed cake when George's maiden aunt, a gentlewoman he had never seen before this day, asked: "What about the female you have under your protection in London?"

He gulped down the rest of his tea, to clear his throat. Then he almost had to bite his tongue to keep from telling this attics-to-let auntie that his affairs were none of her business. Except that he had no affairs, and he was by way of being a guest in her house. "I assure you, madam, that I have no woman in my keeping, in London or elsewhere."

Ty's tone of voice would have frozen a soldier under his command into rigid attention. Miss Linbury clapped her hands. "I knew Mags had to be wrong when she mentioned a girl named Nonny. A fine gentleman like yourself, come to offer—That is, George would never. Or if he did, we never heard of it. Of course, there were those rumors about Clarence and—"

"Nonny is my younger brother, Agamemnon. I might have mentioned that I have to return to London to assist him in a personal matter."

"Your brother, how lovely." She put a second slice of

cake on his plate, then a third, and asked, "So what are your intentions toward my niece?"

While Ty brushed more crumbs off his shirt—he'd need another sleeping powder, dash it, to sleep in this bed tonight—Miss Linbury rattled on: "Nanny and Mindlé and I feel it is my responsibility to ask now that George cannot look out for his sister's interests, and Sir Clarence will not."

The Bible-reading nursemaid, the butler, and this old biddy wanted to know his intentions? Ty would have called out a gentleman for questioning his motives. But this was George's aunt, after all. Besides, perhaps he could get some answers to his own questions.

"My intentions depend entirely on Miss Croft," he said. "Does she need a husband?"

"Oh, yes!"

Miss Linbury's fervency took him aback. It was no more than he expected, but to have his worse fears realized . . .

"And the child?" he had to ask.

Aunt Eliza started to weep once more.

Ty lost his appetite. "No, no. We do not have to speak of it, if the subject is too painful. Please, ma'am."

George's aunt went back to wringing her handkerchief. "Oh, we have all concluded Dilly cannot keep the child. You need not worry on that score. No one would foist— I mean, you don't have to—"

Well, that was a relief, Ty thought, not to have to claim another man's get as his own. Now his debt to George did not have to run counter to his obligation to the St. Ives name. "I will speak to Miss Croft as soon as possible."

Aunt Eliza bobbed her head up and down in approval, sending the red braid into the plate of cake. "Time grows short."

"Indeed. I promised my brother to return to London within the week."

She began to blubber. "Did you promise George to take care of us?"

In horror, Ty watched a tear trail down the lady's lined cheek. "No, I promised myself."

"Oh, you dear, dear boy."

It was bad enough that the old woman threw herself into his arms. Worse, she was weeping on his chest, on the only night raiment he had. Worst of all was that barley water and broth and tea. Ty really had to relieve himself.

Delia helped herself to another slice of toast. "I suppose you are going to tell me to keep away from Tyverne, too?" she asked her aunt while Lizzie buttered her breakfast muffin.

"Oh, no, dear."

Delia's aunt looked almost cheery as she crumbled a slice of bacon for Belinda's dog. Delia was anything but, after half a night at Belinda's bedside. Aunt Eliza had spent part of hers keeping watch over the injured officer, and Delia had been expecting another diatribe. "No? You mean you aren't going to tell me Tyverne is a godless pagan, or a here-and-thereian, just waiting to despoil innocent maidens?"

"La, as if I would use such talk. Perhaps when speaking to myself, which I fear I am wont to do, but never— That is, no, Dilly. Dear Tyverne is none of those things."

"Dear?" Had the major managed to cozen one of her watchdogs?

"A friend of George's, don't you know."

Delia was certain many of George's friends were everything Mags and Nanny labeled Tyverne, and worse. "You're not worried about my reputation or my virtue, then?" she asked, spreading strawberry jam on her toast.

Aunt Eliza took a sip of her tea and sighed her contentment. "No, at last. I trust dear Ty."

"Ty?"

"Yes, such a dear boy. He understands about family. Very devoted to his brother, he is. You should ask him about it, when you speak to him, of course. Perhaps when you're done with your breakfast?" She snatched the last piece of toast off the tray and fed it to the dog. "You were almost finished, weren't you?"

Blessed quiet.

Even better, no one but a young boy was keeping vigil at Ty's bedside when he awoke. He was weak and fuzzy-headed, and his shoulder ached, but Ty thought the worst of the fever had passed. He eyed the boy and the covered tray on the nearby table.

"If that is gruel, be warned that I shall throw the bowl at your head if you come near me with it."

"No, guv'nor, it be Cook's best steak an' kidney pie, what Mr. Mindle ordered special for you, figurin' as how you'd be sharp set. Mr. Mindle, he's our butler."

"And a wise man. I am hungry as a bear. Bring it on, my boy."

The youngster grinned, showing yet another dental divide. This one, Ty decided, was from a missing tooth, not a family trait. The dark-haired boy was watching him intently, ready to hand Ty his knife or a cup of coffee or a mug of ale, obviously under orders to see to the guest's needs. Ty blessed the absent Mindle, and the absence of the Faircroft females. "Who might you be, lad?" he asked the boy between mouthfuls of what had to be the best meal since his return to England.

"Dover, guv."

Ty frowned, so the boy added, "Milord."

"Sir is fine. But Dover, as in the harbor?"

"Right, they named me Dover at the foundling home, Dover Church in full, on account of that's where my mum dropped me an' they were plumb outta names. It's better'n my friend Dusty, what got left in a dustbin."

Ty could sympathize, being encumbered with Archimedes on his own mother's whim.

"And the Crofts took you in?"

Dover beamed with pride. "Miss Dilly, she hired me to be a reg'lar page. That's what she calls it, runnin' errands an' carryin' packages an' helpin' old Mindle. I get to do whatever needs doin'." His grin faded. "When I'm not at school."

"We all have our burdens to bear, Dover. We all have our burdens." Some were heavier than others. Ty put down his fork. "Where do you think Miss Dilly, that is, Miss Croft, is now?"

"Oh, she be at breakfast. I got to show you to the necessary if you can manage, an' then call old Mindle to shave you. I'll make sure to find his spectacles for him, first. An' then, if you're not too tuckered out, I got to tell Miss Eliza, who'll ask Miss Dilly to sit with you while I'm at lessons. Are you really goin' to marry our Miss Dilly?"

Chapter 7

*W*as he going to marry Miss Croft?

That's what Ty had set out to do, when he read Lieutenant Croft's letters in that Portuguese farmhouse. He owed a debt, he saw a need, he made a decision. The problem was, that farmhouse was a long way away, and he was here, in England.

No, the problem was that he had never actually planned on getting married until he'd read of George's sister's dilemma. A soldier could not, should not—and Ty would not—leave dependents behind, or leave half his wits with them at home. As for the succession, Viscount Tyverne had two brothers. Either one would make a better earl, according to the Earl of Stivern himself.

No, that was not the problem, either, Ty admitted to himself. The difficulty was that he did not like women, with all their moods and megrims. He did not understand them, with their fragility and foibles. Hell, the truth was he was terrified of the entire species.

Ty was a military man, not a Town beau. He'd gone from university scholar to soldier without ever going courting, without ever wooing a woman. He had avoided the officers' wives and daughters as being more dangerous than the French, and visited the females of convenience only at his body's insistence. The major was no monk, but he refused to surrender to man's baser instincts, so even those visits were few.

He had scruples.

He had principles.

He had shaking knees.

Mindle mistook the wobbling for remnants of the fever, so the old butler refused to bring his lordship's clothing, and Ty was too wrought to argue. If he was already in bed, Ty reasoned, at least he could not fall at Miss Croft's feet. Again.

The venerable Mindle seemed to understand, for he brought a bit of brandy along with hot water for shaving. Dutch courage be hanged. Ty would take Irish pluck and Russian valor, too, if he had whiskey or vodka.

Washed, shaved, and combed, Ty was as ready as he was ever going to be. He'd faced down the earl, who'd gone into a thundering rage when he learned his heir was going into the army instead of politics, and he'd stood firm against the French. He'd even coped with the three crones of Faircroft House. Surely he could survive Miss Croft and a simple moposal of prarriage. Oh, God.

"Do you know, Mindle, I believe I am feeling warm again. Perhaps I should have that sleeping draught after all."

Too late. The aged retainer was opening the door. "Miss Delia Croft," he announced in formal tones.

Ah, so her name was Delia. At least he would not be wedding something that sounded like a cooking ingredient, Ty noted as he watched the slim woman enter the parlor and cross to his bedside. And his first impression had been correct: Miss Croft was no more pregnant than he was. The crying he had heard hadn't come from an infant, he'd wager, but Aunt Eliza would have mentioned if the child had died. He'd worry about that later. Miss Croft did not smile. He'd worry about the placement of her teeth later, too. For now he'd concentrate on not stammering.

Miss Croft curtsied gracefully, and Ty inclined his head as well as he could manage, propped up among the pillows. She inquired into his health, and he briefly expressed gratitude for her hospitality. She sat on the nearby chair and took up her needlework. He bit the inside of his lip until he could taste blood.

Well, Delia thought, the major certainly had none of the reputed charm of Wellesley's officers. He was as handsome as he could stare, now that the hectic flush had left his complexion, and his eyes were, in fact, a perfect summer-sky blue. Belinda's dog, however, had better manners.

Major Tyverne cleared his throat, and Delia looked up expectantly. She thought he was finally going to explain his presence and his extraordinary proposition. Instead, the officer cleared his throat again.

"Do you need a drink? Shall I ask Mindle to bring tea?"

Not unless the old man laced it with nightshade this time, Ty thought. Brandy was simply not going to do the job. He shook his head. "No." Lud, what if he had to use the necessary? "No thank you."

Delia sighed. The guest was as conversable as he was convenient. She had other matters to attend to this morning, so said, "Perhaps you would tell me about George."

Lud, Ty thought, what if she cried? He eyed the stack of handkerchiefs the estimable Mindle had placed near his bedside. No, there was not time enough to knot them into a noose to hang himself. Still, this was George's sister. She had the right to know, and she did not seem the vaporish sort. Not yet, at any rate.

So he told Miss Croft about the battle and the retreat, how her dashing brother had ridden through a cloud of dust and despair to save his life. The telling loosened his tongue, although recalling the lieutenant's final gap-toothed smile almost trapped the words in Ty's throat. Miss Croft's eyes—pretty green eyes, he noted—filled with tears, but she did not turn into a watering pot, thank goodness.

Then she asked how her brother had died. She was George's sister, he told himself again, she had the right to know. So he lied. He talked about bravery and skill, and a quick, painless death.

When Miss Croft helped herself to one of the linen squares and blew her nose, Ty said, "So you see what a great debt I owe your brother."

"Why, no, sir, I do not. He was a soldier at war. Coming to the aid of one's fallen comrades must be part of an officer's duties. You would have done the same for him, would you have not?"

"Of course. But I never had the opportunity. Your brother did, so the debt is mine. It is a matter of honor, you see." He was certain she did not see. Women seldom understood codes of gentlemanly behavior or the ethics of war.

She nodded, though, as if she accepted his interpretation. "And so that is why you are here?"

Ty was relieved. A reasonable woman, after all, was George's sister. "Yes."

"To . . . ?"

Dash it, he thought, she was going to make him say it! He swallowed once, twice, then said, "I am here to offer for your hand in matrimony, Miss Croft, if you would do me the honor." There, he'd gotten the words out without a single missed syllable, just as he'd been practicing for the last fortnight. He must have given a sigh of relief, for the woman frowned.

"Why," she asked after a moment's deliberation, "do you think I would take a stranger as husband?"

In all of Ty's rehearsals, Croft's sister had thanked him for the honor of his offer, and agreed to make him the happiest of men. Now he'd be happy if the ground opened up. Feeling a warm flush that had nothing to do with fever spread across his cheeks, he confessed to reading her letter. "I felt it was necessary, to ensure the well-being of Lieutenant Croft's dependents."

Delia stabbed her needle into the fabric she was stitching. "And when you read that we were at point-non-plus, you decided to ride *ventre à terre* to present yourself as the sacrificial lamb."

"That was, ah, not precisely as I would have expressed the situation."

"No? You did not gallop straight here from your sickbed—"

He interrupted. "I stopped in Canterbury for a special license."

"—to immolate yourself on the pyre of wedlock?" Delia pulled her needle so hard she snapped the thread.

He should have known she would not understand. What woman could? "I saw it as a matter of honor, as I said, a debt to be repaid."

"If you felt you owed George a debt, why did you not offer us financial assistance? A loan or something?"

"My knowledge of the social niceties might be deficient, but my understanding is that an exchange of money between an unmarried lady and a gentleman is tantamount to an acceptance of a proposal—or a slip on the shoulder."

Now it was Delia's turn to blush. "Quite. I would not have accepted monies, even if you had claimed a gambling debt to George."

Ty wished he'd thought of that, but no amount of brass could restore a woman's reputation. He watched as she fussed with her sewing. Surely that was an infant's gown Miss Croft was stitching, so all the weeping and praying had not been for a lost child. He'd need to make arrangements: formalize his guardianship, establish an annuity, locate a decent family. It was somewhat like finding a good home for one's favorite old pony.

The ordinary act of rethreading her needle restored Delia's composure. "Tell me, my lord"—somehow, discussing Tyverne's patronizing, pompous, and presumptuous proposal made him more the viscount, less the military man—"do you *wish* to get married? It seems to me that you must have had any number of opportunities, had you so desired."

"I have certain family obligations that make taking a wife at this time desirable," he extemporized. "The succession and such."

"Yet you became a soldier without worrying over carrying on your line." It was more an accusation than a question.

"I had two brothers."

"Had?"

Dash it, Ty wondered, was this a court-martial or a marriage proposal? He loosened the cloth Mindle had tied around his neck to make him more presentable for lady callers. "I still have two brothers, Miss Croft, yet now I see where my own duty lies."

"A duty such as marriage to me would be?"

He nodded.

"A duty fulfilled and a repayment of your debt to George for your life at the same time?"

There, she did understand! "Precisely."

Delia gave up on her sewing before she mangled the little gown beyond repair—or stuck her needle in this dolt's big toe, tempting under the nearby covers. The clunch did not begin to comprehend how a woman might be insulted to be seen in the light of a debt or duty. Still, watching his lordship struggle like a trout on the line was almost worth the aggravation. Not that Delia was a cruel woman, just that she'd reached the end of her tether. She needed a miracle, not a muddleheaded, misguided moron who thought he was doing her a favor.

Because his motives were honorable—hen-witted, but honorable—she did not storm out of the room. Instead, she asked, "Why do you not tell me about your brothers?"

Ty sighed. The woman was worse than a weasel with a rat. Now that she'd stopped sewing, Miss Croft was giving Ty her full attention. That cold green-eyed gaze could freeze a man in his boots, if he were wearing any. "We were, ah, four siblings. Three boys and a girl. I am the eldest."

"Archimedes."

Ty grimaced and muttered something unsuitable for a stable, much less a lady's presence. "How the deuce . . . ? Oh, my papers."

"We had to read them when you fell," she echoed sweetly, "to see if you had dependents nearby."

Ty went back to chewing on his lip. After a moment or two, Delia said, "I suppose the boys at school called you Archie?"

"Only once. I was always big for my size, and strong. I was born a viscount, Tyverne, so that is what I am called. Totty—Aristotle—comes next, then Nonny, whose actual name is Agamemnon. Our mother died giving birth to our sister."

"Goodness, Alcestes? Alcmene? Ariadne?"

"Ann. Mother was the one with the classical leanings, not my sire. The earl happened to be around for that birth, and the countess's death, so he had the naming of the infant."

That seemed all the viscount had to say on the matter, although what he had not said piqued Delia's interest. After another silence, she asked, "Is it not unusual for the eldest son to take up colors?"

"If you must know"—and he supposed she must, if they were to wed. Miss Croft would hear the story quickly enough when they went to London—"my father and I do not get along." And that was as much of an understatement as calling the war against Napoleon a skirmish.

"Oh?"

Oh, hell.

Chapter 8

T he deuced woman wanted more. They always did. By strength of will alone did Ty keep from squirming on the bed like a recalcitrant three-year-old. Bad enough the blasted female hadn't simply accepted his eminently sensible—and spotlessly executed, if Tyverne had to say so himself—proposal. Worse that she was putting him through the Spanish Inquisition. Worst of all, this dogged determination to have his privates on a platter did not bode well for a comfortable marriage. Not at all. Viscount Tyverne never spoke about his father, not to anyone. Ever.

"Your father?"

He closed his eyes. "My father wished me to marry the young woman of his choice, the daughter of a duke who had no other heir. The court was to be petitioned to combine the titles, and the fortunes, of course. She was fifteen. I was nineteen. I refused."

"Good for you!"

He opened his eyes to give her a disgruntled look. "My father cut me off without a shilling. I stayed at university on a loan against expectations, and by tutoring other boys. I also had a small sum set aside, from my godfather. The duke's wife died some years later, and he remarried within three months, with hopes of a male heir." Ty scowled at the memory. "His daughter ran off with an Irish groom while he was on honeymoon."

"Good for her."

"How could living in a thatch-roofed cottage on potatoes and cabbage be good for her?"

"If it was what she wanted—"

"She wanted to avoid marriage to me if I could be coerced into it, if her new stepmother failed to provide the requisite son."

"And then?"

"Then the earl tried to convince me to wed another woman of his choice, promising to restore my income. He was now determined that I enter politics, envisioning his heir a member of the cabinet at least. A properly advantageous marriage would further Stivern's ambitions for me, and that young lady's father was a leader in Parliament. I almost agreed. University life was growing tiresome. So was penury."

"But you did not."

"I did not. The earl had plans for all of his children. Totty, the second son, was to go into the army. Totty, however, is a gentle soul who is only happy around horses. He lives and breathes them. All he ever wished to do was breed horses, not see them killed in a cavalry charge. Stivern did not care; Totty was going to fight for his country. I reasoned, however, that if I signed up instead, Father would never jeopardize his spare heir. I bought my commission the day I attained my majority. I repaid my loans, sent the duke's daughter and her Irish husband a bank draft as a belated wedding gift, and gave Totty money to purchase a farm in the Colonies. He swears he will never come home."

Delia could not help being impressed by this man's generosity, and his strength of purpose. Nothing, it seemed, could force him down a road not of his choice, nor deter him from the path he had selected. She supposed those must be excellent traits in an officer, if not a husband. "What about your youngest brother?"

"Nonny was intended for the clergy. He is a natural farmer, but Stivern decided that estate management was beneath the dignity of an earl's son, so he kept him nearly cloistered. The boy turned out to be a hell-raker, of course." He held up his hand. "And do not say good for him. When he was permanently sent down from school, Nonny fell into bad habits, with a bad crowd of London bloods. Now he is about to make a bad connection. He is too young and too useless to make his own way, and, frankly, too expensive for me to support, despite the easy competence I currently enjoy. Nonny is part of the reason I hurried here. The gudgeon swore not to do anything rash, like fly to Gretna Green, before I returned."

"So you would all have fled your father's authority? You to the army, one brother to the Colonies and the other to a too hasty wedding?"

"We do not sound like dutiful sons, do we? Nor men of steadfast character, either."

She did not answer. "What of your sister?" she asked instead.

"I could do least for her, having no legal authority. My father betrothed her to the widowed duke, the one whose daughter I was to wed, on the night of Ann's come-out ball. They were wed a month later."

Delia was horrified. "The duke must be ancient!"

"Young enough to have hopes for a male heir off an eighteen-year-old girl."

"Your father forced her . . . ?"

He snorted.

"Of course. No girl would willingly pick a man more than twice her age."

Ty was thinking of that Baron Dallsworth, Miss Croft's erstwhile suitor. He was trying not to think of the father of the child, and if he were worth killing. He was no Sir Snoop, though, not like his hostess. He'd ask Mindle.

"Forgive me," she was saying now, "but he does not sound like a pleasant man, your father."

The earl was as pleasant as an asp. "Oh, we'd never have to see him, if that is what you fear. Stivern has not left Warwickshire in ages, and I have a few bits of property in my own name."

Ignoring the viscount's litany of estates, hunting boxes,

and unused town houses, Delia was thinking that she did not fear meeting the Earl of Stivern at all. In fact, she'd love to give that martinet a piece of her mind, for ruining his children's lives. No, what she did fear was that this already commanding officer would turn into just such a domestic despot. He was large and loud, and used to giving orders. He'd make some poor woman an awful husband. Some other poor woman, thank goodness.

"Tell me," she asked. "Did your parents have an arranged marriage?"

More personal questions? The woman was relentless. At this rate, they'd be here till next August, while she asked about his favorite color! Ty could think of a few traits he'd like less than incessant curiosity in a wife— very few. A vaporish female would be horrid, a giggler almost as bad. He did not think he could tolerate a fashion plate, a flirt, or a screeching soprano. Miss Croft was none of those, thank heavens.

Ty knew little of women's styles, but he knew Miss Croft's sack-like black gown fit no fashion. It did not even fit Miss Croft. Beyond the gown she was passably pretty, if one did not mind red hair and a scattering of freckles across her cheeks. She was too pale and too thin, but he supposed those defects could be altered, while an argumentative nature could not be. Her voice was soft and pleasant, though, when she was not harping on matters that did not concern her.

"Your parents?" Delia repeated.

"Oh. Yes, theirs was an arranged marriage. Most were, in those days, more so than now. It was deemed an advantageous match by both families, I understand."

"And were they happy, your mother and father?"

Ty could see that Miss Croft was steering them toward dangerous waters. He merely shook his head no. "From what I recall. She died early."

"No, I would not have assumed so, from what you said of your father. My parents, however, married to please themselves, without being concerned with property or power. They enjoyed almost every moment they had together. That is the kind of marriage I wish for myself."

Ty knew it. He just knew the female was going to start nattering on about true love and grand passion. He thought he might manage to enjoy some of his time with Miss Croft, if she kept her mouth shut. "We cannot always have what we want," he answered in a repressive tone, hoping to halt any more romantical drivel.

"No," Delia agreed, "but we can avoid, sometimes, that which we do *not* want. I can think of nothing worse than being trapped in a loveless marriage."

"Respect is a worthy bond."

"I respect the archbishop, yet I have no wish to be wed to him."

Ty started chewing on the inside of his lip again, blast the woman. "Affection can grow, with time."

Delia feared she might indeed grow fond of this handsome hero—right before he left for another battle. "What if affection did not follow the nuptials?"

"Then we could maintain separate residences. Lord knows my parents did. They spent so little time in each other's company, it is a marvel they had four children. I would never force my presence on you, I swear."

"Then what about that heir you seek?"

"As I said, we cannot always have everything we wish for."

Delia gathered her sewing and stood to leave. "No, my lord, we cannot. And so I wish you a good morning and a speedy recovery."

That was it? She was refusing his offer out of hand because Ty did not profess eternal devotion? Hell and damnation. "Halt! Ah, that is, please wait." When she paused, one hand on the door, which had been left partially open for propriety's sake, he tried a different tack. "Will you at least consider my offer for a day? That's how long before I can get a message to the man I left in Canterbury with my baggage, to hire a carriage and come fetch me here."

Delia hovered where she was. "I shall not change my mind."

"Have you a better option? I could leave more easily knowing your future was secure. Baron Dallsworth . . . ?"

"How do you— That is, I do not believe that my future is any of your concern, my lord."

Dash it, Ty swore to himself, his dastard of a father was none of her affair, yet Miss Croft had not hesitated to probe that wound like a surgeon for a pistol ball. When they married, she would have to learn that a man kept certain matters private. But they were not going to marry, were they?

Of course they were, Ty assured himself. Delia Croft was a reasonable person, for a female. She seemed a tad given to flights of fancy, but this had to be an emotional time for her. Given a day's reflection, George's sister would come to see that his was the best offer she was likely to receive. Ty knew he was Miss Croft's finest chance of seeing the child well situated, and her other dependents, her old Nanny and Aunt Eliza, comfortably fixed. He thanked providence for those minor properties of his, where he could lodge any number of bothersome relatives and retainers. George's sister was sure to see the benefits of his proposal, too, with time. That would be another day wasted while Miss Croft came to her senses, and who knew what mischief Nonny could get up to in the meantime, but Ty felt he had no choice.

"Please," he repeated. "Just think about my offer. I cannot walk away until you do. My honor will not permit me."

Delia still held the doorknob, hoping the viscount could not see the white knuckles of her hand. The devil take him and his offer! "This is all about honor, isn't it?"

They'd been over this ground. "Without honor a man has nothing."

"What does a woman have, then?"

"A woman's virtue is her honor. She wears her reputation as a man wears his sword. With the protection of my ring and my title, your good name is restored." He let his gaze drift to the sewing bag she held and the infant's gown it contained.

"I do not accept your reasoning, my lord. I care little for my reputation, but much for my sense of fairness. My principles, my own understanding of right and wrong, will not permit me to inflict myself and my burdens on a man who did nothing more than live through a battle others did not survive. No, *my* honor will not permit me to accept an offer made out of obligation."

Ty could taste defeat. No, that was the blood, from him gnawing on his lip. "What of my debt to George, then?"

"Ah, your debt. I would consider every iota of it repaid in full if you hurry to get well, and remove your wretched horse from my stable."

"What, has Diablo been a bother?"

"A bother? Now, how could you think that?" she asked with a smile. "He's only cost me two bonnets, one groom who resigned, a parasol, a fortune in sweets from the apothecary, and Cook's services. No bother, my lord."

She'd smiled at last. Not for him, but for the damned horse, yet Ty felt as if he'd defeated Napoleon single-handedly. The smile transformed Miss Croft's whole face, making her seem younger, more like the carefree lass she should have been, a sunbeam to warm a soldier's heart. And she did have a tiny gap between her front teeth, a charming, saucy space. Ty wondered what that opening would feel like against his tongue.

Now where had that thought come from?

Chapter 9

*I*n the end, Delia agreed to consider Viscount Tyverne's offer, in light of the light in his light blue eyes. Besides, she was not going to be thinking of anything else but his preposterous proposal anyway.

Delia was not going to change her mind. No matter how many advantages she could see in the match, she would not accept a suitor in scarlet regimentals. She was still dealing with the detritus of the last dashing soldier in the neighborhood.

Aunt Eliza was weeping, of course, having already counted the benefits of the connection, and recognizing none of the drawbacks. She knew of her niece's rejection of Tyverne's offer as soon as Tyverne, what with Mindle stationed outside the partially open door. Even the valet-turned-butler was giving Delia reproving looks. Of course. Their futures with the viscount would be rosier than the bed of thorns Sir Clarence was apt to offer.

Escaping her minions' disappointment, Delia went out to the stables to visit Diablo. She thought that one creature, at least, might understand her affront at being handed along from man to man, as if she were . . . a horse. Perhaps Diablo could not comprehend her dismay at being considered part payment of a debt, just another bit of George's bequeathal to be administered, but the horse did not frown or whimper. He was too busy shredding her least favorite bonnet, the one she was too embarrassed to donate to the church needy box. She'd brought it along in case the horse was bored with bon-bons, now that he had one less groom to terrorize.

His ears flickering to the changes in her voice, Diablo was a good listener. He only kicked the wall once, when Delia pounded her fist into the gate, recalling the viscount's calm assurance that he was the answer to this maiden's prayers.

He was well-off if not wealthy, and generous with his funds, it seemed. From a prominent family, with an eminent career, he was attractive, educated, and honorable to a fault. The man was most likely a certified hero, by Jupiter, and Delia still wanted none of him.

She had never sought title or *ton*, wealth or recognition. She certainly never aspired to become a viscountess, much less a countess with countless houses and chests full of jewels. All Delia wished was the loving comfort of a family of her own, something Viscount Tyverne could never offer, if he knew such a thing existed. Perhaps he did not, with his upbringing. But Delia did. She was twenty-one years old, and she still had her dreams. George had never given up. Why should she?

She tried not to consider that Aunt Lizzie might have dreams, too. Even Mindle might have aspirations for his old age. Cousin Clarence and his wife would never keep the aged retainer, though. His stooped gait and spectacles would not suit their new self-consequence. Nor would they feel duty-bound to pension him and Nanny off. George, the cabbage-head, had thought he'd live forever. There was no will that Delia could find, to prove that he'd made provision for any of them.

"If that jackanapes hadn't gone and gotten himself killed," she told his horse, "I would be tempted to murder him myself."

Well, she'd just have to figure something out when this other mess was done. Granted, she had not come up with a decent solution yet, but she would, and it would not involve a marriage of convenience that was sure to be deucedly inconvenient.

When the sweets and the hat were equally demolished,

Delia knew she had to return to the house. She would much rather go for a ride, a fast ride, astride, in George's old britches, the way she used to, but she was older now, in mourning, with heavy responsibilities resting on her shoulders. She could never outride her problems, no matter how fast the steed. Besides, the room she'd given the viscount overlooked the stable yard, and Delia did not wish him to think her a graceless hoyden. Furthermore, she was out of brandied sugar cubes.

Reluctantly heading back toward the house, Delia thanked her lucky stars that she had not given into temptation, for a carriage was pulled up in front of the door. She recognized the coach easily, as well she might since the vehicle had belonged to Faircroft House not three months past. The carriage still did, of course, but Cousin Clarence now owned both. The furor that would have erupted if he and Gwen had espied her in britches did not bear contemplating. Neither did the reason for their visit.

She should not be surprised to see her relatives, Delia told herself, not once news of the viscount's arrival reached their ears. A titled gentleman in the vicinity, a respectable, rich gentleman, was sure to bring them running like ants to a picnic—or vultures to a wounded beast.

The viscount was resting, Mindle reported, sparing Delia the embarrassment of having to present two of the biggest toads in the Hillsdale-at-Hythe pond. Fortunate man, she told herself. Or wise on the butler's advice.

She called for tea, hoping Cook had managed to prepare something, between cooking for the sickroom, for heroically proportioned gentlemen, and for their horses. Clarence would eat the rugs, otherwise. Clarence was not running to fat; he had outdistanced it years ago. Gwen, who was perpetually watching her weight—watching it increase with every sugarplum she popped in her mouth—was sure to disdain whatever appeared from Faircroft's country kitchens.

She'd been wrong, Delia realized as she waited for the

tea cart to be brought. Her relations had not sacrificed their scruples to come here in order to fawn over the viscount for the afternoon. They came to complain that they could not move in, to fawn over him for as long as he stayed. A viscount, a wounded hero, Cousin Clarence declared at his wife's prompting, ought to be entertained as befitted his stature.

No matter that his stature was laid out on a makeshift bed in the room next door, Gwen wanted to hold a dinner party in his honor, here at Faircroft. The neighbors would expect it.

"What," Delia asked, "you'd throw a celebratory party in George's house, with him barely cold in his grave?" Gwen was wearing a rose carriage dress under her furs, with a black ribbon wound through the ecru lace at the straining neckline. Clarence had on a puce and primrose striped waistcoat that did not button across his girth, a black armband his only sop to mourning.

Gwen pulled her fur tippet closer to her ample bosom, like a ferret on a shelf. "Unlike others I could mention, we are well aware of the proprieties. We would not have dancing, of course."

"I am afraid that is impossible. His lordship is too ill"—Delia crossed her fingers behind her back, to make sure she did not jinx the viscount's recovery—"and the staff cannot possibly manage a gathering at this time, with invalids in the house." Aunt Eliza nodded her agreement from the stiff-backed chair she'd chosen, as far from the sofa the usurpers shared as possible. They, in turn, ignored Delia's aunt completely. Delia continued: "As for your rooms, you agreed about Belinda."

"We agreed on a temporary visit. You said you were going to do something about That Person."

Clarence's voice was taking on the same petulant tone he always had as a child, when the macaroons were gone. Delia prayed Mindle would hurry with the refreshments. "Yes, I was making plans for Belinda," she told her cousins, full knowing all her ideas had expired with George. If her fingers were crossed any tighter, she would not be able to pour out the tea when it finally arrived. "But now she is too ill to move. I explained that in my letter."

Gwen sniffed. "I am sure she is not too ill to remove to the attics. I bore all three of my children without inconveniencing anyone. She belongs in the attics, if not the stables. Not," she said with another sniff and another twitch to the beady-eyed beastie dead on her breast, "in the baronet's suite."

"But then Nanny, Aunt Eliza, Mags, and I would be climbing those narrow stairs constantly. No, it will not fadge. Furthermore, it would be unnecessary. His lordship is most likely leaving on the morrow."

Gwen screeched. "What, before we get to meet him?" She jumped up and began rearranging the figurines on the mantel. "No, if he was as ill as we heard, then he must stay on at least a sennight. And we must be here as hosts."

Delia supposed moving the furniture around was Gwen's right now, but the collection of china dogs on the mantel had been her mother's, not part of the entailment at all. So she answered a bit more caustically than she ought, perhaps, knowing how sensitive Gwen was to her roots in trade. "Tyverne *must*? Who are you to give orders to an earl's son?"

"Pish-tosh, he will enjoy the attention. Every man does."

Tyverne did not seem the sort to enjoy being fussed over, but Delia held her tongue. Gwen did not. "And what are you thinking of, anyway, my girl? You need us here to lend you countenance. Consider your reputation, for once, and how it reflects on us."

"What reputation?" Delia asked. "You swore mine was destroyed when I gave Belinda comfort after her father threw her out of his house."

"But George was alive then, and we had no say in the matter."

They had said a great deal, however, all of it ugly, unfair, and unhelpful.

Gwen paused in her assessment of the knickknacks to

resume her seat next to Clarence, and next to the dish
of sherried ginger biscuits Mindle had brought in. Delia
hoped they enjoyed them. The horse had not.

Gwen wrinkled her long nose at the biscuits, but
deigned to try one, before Clarence could devour them
all. "Still, that was then, and you promised it was a temporary arrangement. Your reputation might have recovered. But now we say—"

She pinched Clarence's arm, so he put down the second pastry he was holding and said, "Right. Now we
say . . . what?"

"That a single gentleman in the house of an unmarried
female is shocking."

Clarence took another bite. "Quite. Dallsworth complained to me when he got wind of it."

Delia started to point to Aunt Eliza as chaperone
enough, when another thought struck her. "Dallsworth?
What does that old reprobate's opinion matter?"

Clarence puffed out his cheeks. Likely so he could
stuff more biscuits in. "Fine gentleman, Dallsworth. Well
respected, don't you know."

Delia knew he pinched the housemaids every chance
he got. She busied herself fixing the tea Mindle finally
brought. She thought of asking Gwen to pour, since Clarence's wife was nominally hostess. But that was Delia's
mother's Wedgwood on the tray, and Delia's temper
under the thinnest control. She poured.

Gwen examined the slices of bread and butter presented,
looked down her long nose, and refused. "Dallsworth is
the highest-ranking gentleman of the neighborhood," she
reminded Delia, as if Delia had ever been allowed to forget. He also had the rankest breath in the neighborhood,
Tom Burdock's prize hog notwithstanding.

His mouth full, and both of his hands, Clarence managed to say, "He's agreed to renew his suit."

Delia almost spilled her tea. "He is taking you to
court?"

"Haw!" Clarence guffawed crumbs across his vividly
striped waistcoat, and the damask sofa. "Told you our

Dilly was a right 'un. Still, it don't look good, my girl," he admonished, waving a finger of toast at her, "entertaining another gent."

Delia put down her mother's teacup before she was tempted to toss it at her cousin's head. "The viscount is ill, as you well know, so I am not entertaining anyone. Furthermore, I am absolutely not entertaining Dallsworth's suit. Not now, not ever. We have been over this before, cousin, with the same results."

"But that was when you had other choices," Clarence said, deliberating between the bread and butter or the ginger biscuits. "You've got none left, Dilly. Asides, we gave you time to get over your grief, and this other do-good nonsense. Now you have to marry. You must see that."

"I do not see that at all." Delia could see where Clarence and Gwen would not want her in their home, but that did not mean she had to wed.

"Well, I am in charge now," Clarence insisted. "And I say you will accept Dallsworth."

She tried to make light of his command. Her cousin, after all, was her legal guardian, trustee of her funds. "What, Clarence, are you going to drag me, kicking and screaming, to the altar? That's the only way I would get there, you know, and I still would not repeat my vows. What, to honor and obey a man who picks his teeth in public?"

Clarence sputtered, and put his penknife back in his pocket.

"But why are you two so keen on Dallsworth's suit," Delia wondered out loud, "especially with another eligible gentleman so suddenly in our midst?"

"Dash it, girl," Clarence shouted. "It ain't for you to question me."

"What, did he promise you a patronage position in exchange for my dowry? An apartment in his London town house? Are you to profit by the marriage settlements?" Delia's own voice was raised now. "What is it,

Clarence, that you have to gain by my wedding that wantwit?"

Clarence turned an unattractive shade of purple, especially next to his lurid waistcoat, and Gwen said, "Nonsense. Remember your place, girl."

"I have no place, remember? But I will not help you, whatever your self-serving motives. I am not going to marry that—"

"Of course you are not going to marry Mr. Dallsworth, my dear Miss Croft" came in firm tones from the doorway. "You are going to marry me."

Two teacups—and Gwen—hit the rug at the same time.

Chapter 10

*A*fter Miss Croft left him, Ty sank back on his pillows, exhausted. Twenty minutes in the female's company was like a month of fevers. He must have drowsed, for he awoke to weeping and moaning again. Lud, was his proposal so offensive? No, he recalled, both sounds seemed perpetual in this house. He would have gone to investigate except that most of the noises seemed to be coming from the family rooms, above, where he had no possible excuse for exploring. Then he heard shouting, from much closer by. The argument was going on in the next room, in fact, unless he missed his guess. The words were coming so clearly, Ty did not consider himself an eavesdropper as much as an unwilling audience—until he heard his name mentioned.

Someone was yelling at Ty's Miss Croft, for that was how he considered her. He also considered that, while he might wish to shake some sense into Delia's pretty red head, no one else had the right to disturb one of those bright curls. From what he could gather, Clarence, the cousin mentioned in George's letters, was decidedly disturbing her peace of mind.

Ty jumped out of bed, then steadied himself and his reeling senses against a side table. Still unsteady, he grabbed his pantaloons from the back of a chair and pulled them on. He tucked George's nightshirt down the waist as best he could, then struggled into his uniform coat. His boots were missing, taken off by Mindle and

Dover so the boy could learn how a gentleman's foot-wear was properly polished. He missed his sword more than the boots as he followed the sound of the angry voices. Blasted civilian life!

Sir Clarence's speech was growing louder as he threat-ened Miss Croft with Dallsworth. Ty was truly beginning to despise the merest mention of that man's name, and he did not think much of the new baronet, either. Even Ty knew that planting him a facer in the lady's parlor could not be considered polite, so there was only one thing for him to do. He threw open the parlor door and announced, "Of course you are not going to marry Dalls-worth, my dear Miss Croft. You are going to marry me."

Brilliant tactics, Ty congratulated himself, spiking the enemy's guns and reinforcing his own position at the same time. Ty was particularly proud of remembering to put in the "my dear" to appeal to Miss Croft's roman-tical bent.

Perhaps he should have considered his strategy a bit more, he thought, when he saw the effect of his state-ment. Hell, he should have drawn Clarence's claret—if the tub of lard now gaping at him like a landed trout was indeed George's cousin—and been done with it. Lud knew no one would have noticed, against that waistcoat.

Miss Croft, it seemed, was not impressed with Ty's battle plan. "I am not going to marry anyone!" she shouted as she bent first to pick up the crockery, and then find Gwen's smelling salts in her reticule.

Delicate dishes and fainting females were two of Ty's terrors. He stayed rooted by the door, as horror-stricken as the chaw-bacon Clarence, if for different reasons.

Delia glared at both of them as she had to drag a barely revived Gwen back onto the sofa by herself. After she'd placed a fresh cup of tea in the woman's hand—in a fresh, unchipped teacup—and another in Aunt Eliza's, who was quietly weeping in the corner, possibly out of joy, she stormed at Tyverne. "Now see what you have done."

What had he done? Saved her from being browbeaten

into matrimony with a man she evidently despised? Or worse, from a life of shame and scrimping? Worst yet, having to live with these mushrooms and their undoubtedly spore-like offspring? Ty shrugged. "I announced our engagement a bit prematurely, is all."

"We had no engagement, you big oaf!"

"I heard him say it, Dilly," Clarence put in, flapping his handkerchief in Gwen's face until she slapped it away.

The viscount examined his fingers. "Do you know, I am not fond of pet names. I suppose that's natural, with an appellation like Archimedes, but I find they remind me of pets, or little brothers."

Miss Croft looked at Ty as if he were insane. "What has that to do with anything, for Heaven's sake?"

But Clarence understood. "Why do you not introduce us, uh, Delia?"

So she did, and Gwen even managed a simper, before Delia impatiently told them to ignore anything Lord Tyverne said. "The man is obviously ranting, out of his mind with fever. Why, he even forgot his shoes."

Ty looked down at his bare feet and wiggled his toes in the carpet. "No, Mindle has my boots for polishing."

"I doubt that old relic will know the proper way to go about it," Clarence began. "Now my valet has a secret formula—"

Ty studied the older man's overstuffed ensemble. He wished, for once, that he had a quizzing glass, a London dandy's affectation, so he could raise it now, to depress this toadstool's pretensions. He made do with saying, "Yes, I can see that your man is a dab hand at dressing a gentleman."

Miss Croft made an unladylike noise, but Gwen had revived enough after the tea to pinch her husband's arm and whisper in his ear.

Ty was wishing someone would offer him tea or, better, a brandy. His head was beginning to ache again, and his legs were still not steady.

"What? What? Oh, yes, Dilly. I mean Delia. That is,

you cannot be engaged to our cousin, Tyverne. I never gave permission."

"Ah, but I had it from her guardian." He reached into his pocket for a folded paper, which he held out to Delia. "I have it here, in Lieutenant Croft's last letter, which he never got to post. I meant to give it to you earlier, my dear, but forgot while I was on my sickbed."

Clarence heaved himself off the sofa. "Here, I'll take that."

"What, you'd read Miss Croft's personal mail, the last she will have from her beloved brother?" Ty asked, swearing to himself to purchase a quizzing glass at the next opportunity. "I think not."

Clarence sank back, defeated. He brightened when he spotted the last slice of buttered toast.

Delia, meanwhile, had begged the others' pardons and stepped away to read the letter. She would study it later, and likely weep over George's final words to her, but skimmed it quickly now. Ty, meanwhile, poured himself a cup of tea and commandeered the toast.

When she was finished reading, Delia looked up and said, "But this says nothing about—"

"Waiting. I know," Tyverne told her. "That is why I procured a special license on my way here." He patted another coat pocket. Then he turned to Gwen, Lady Croft. "I thought a simple ceremony, just the family and closest friends, because of our recent loss. I am sure you would know better the proper form for these things, while honoring George's wishes."

"George did not—" Delia began, only to find her mouth full of toast.

Clarence was shaking his head. "George never did have a particle of sense. Going off to war half-cocked when there was no need."

Ty suddenly lost his appetite for tea. "There was every need, for each and every brave lad."

"I'll grant you brave, but my cousin was nothing but a hey-go-mad hellion."

His wife nodded, the stuffed head of the poor dead

creature bobbing on her chest. "Just look at the mess he left."

"He left me alive to remedy the situation." Ty drew himself up to his considerable height, in formidable, rigid military stance despite his weakened state. "Lieutenant Croft, your cousin Sir George, saved my life. That is enough."

Clarence waved a fleshy hand in the air. "Right, right. No need to get in a taking, I say. Oughtn't speak ill of the dead at any rate. Still and all, George never told *me* his wishes, so you cannot marry Dilly. Um, Delia. I gave her hand to Dallsworth."

Ty looked down at the woman next to him. He saw two delicate appendages formed into serviceable fists. "These do not seem taken," he said, taking both of them into his much larger hands before Miss Croft could decide to use them. "Nor do I see a ring on any finger."

Delia tried to wrench her hands away, a futile endeavor for sure, considering the viscount-major's superior size, strength, and determination to outmaneuver Clarence. Her color was heightened, Ty noted, although not as high as near apoplectic Clarence's, nor the shade of his wife's, who was in a pinkish gown more suited for a young girl—a thin young girl.

While Delia kept struggling to free her hands, Ty decided that the added color made Miss Croft deuced attractive. Not as pretty as when she smiled, of course, but vibrant, alive, alluring, especially with her red hair coming out of its neat coil to curl around her cheeks. Besides, he was coming to admire her spirit.

To avoid creating more of a scene than he already had, Ty let go of one of Miss Croft's hands, but he kept the other. It felt right here, just the right size and softness. He was enjoying the feel of her smooth, ungloved skin in his so much, in fact, that he brought it to his lips.

She stomped on his feet. His bare feet. Perhaps a bit less spirit would be a bit more admirable.

Clarence was still sputtering. "And you could not have

her anyway, not without my permission, because she is still underage."

"Ah, but I thought a special license was for just such eventualities."

The special license meant age or permission or reading of the banns were all unnecessary, and Clarence knew it. With that document in hand, Delia could wed the devil himself, or the linen draper. "But . . . but I do not have to release her dowry, if she marries against my will."

"Oh, did you have a dowry, my dear?" Ty asked Delia, as if such a thought had never occurred to him, which, in all honesty, it had not. Money was not important here, not to him, at any rate. "I assure you I will not miss it." He squeezed her hand slightly when she would have spoken, then addressed her cousin: "But tell me, Sir Clarence, do you intend to refuse my suit? That is, if I do decide I should ask you, despite having the lady's brother's approval."

"Of course I will deny you. Already gave the nod to Dallsworth, I said."

Ty ignored mention of his would-be rival. "Now that I think on it, Miss Croft's dowry would be welcome, to settle on any daughters the match might produce. Sons, naturally, will be handsomely provided for from the estate. I wonder how you would explain that to my solicitors, withholding your blessings, and the dower monies, from a marriage between your cousin and a St. Ives. The St. Ives heir, in fact. You are not questioning my ability to support Miss Croft in fitting manner, I assume." His gaze traveled around the parlor, which, while neater and grander than most of his recent army billets, would have fit inside the entry halls of half his father's houses. "One can only gather, therefore, that you are finding fault with my character."

This last was spoken softly, not so much a statement as a challenge. Ty might have tossed a glass of wine in the baronet's choleric face, if he had a glass of wine, or slapped Clarence's rounded cheeks with his glove, if he was wearing any. Instead, he skewered the corpulent coxcomb with his blue-eyed stare. "I think that would be a mistake."

Croft's wife was clutching his arm, wrinkling the fabric and possibly saving her husband's life. "You cannot do it, Clarence. His father is an earl. Tyverne will be an earl someday. You cannot refuse a viscount's offer."

"Well, I can!" Delia said, finally reclaiming her hand and pointedly wiping it on her skirt and hoping the tingling would go away. "I can and do."

Aunt Eliza started weeping again. Ty knew it was time to drag out the heavy artillery. He was growing weary and weaker, and losing the war, although he might have defeated Clarence in the day's battle. "I'd wager Dallsworth is not willing to accept the child."

Five mouths hung open, including Mindle's, who had returned with the major's boots. Delia regained the use of her senses first. "And you are?"

Ty had been thinking. No woman wanted to give up her baby, he had reasoned, no matter how it was conceived, so George's sister might be more amenable to his suit if that offer included her child. Taking the infant into his home would generate gossip, but what did he care? Many well-known families had irregular entries in their pedigrees, and Ty did not care if they lived away from London, where rumormongers and scandal-brewers thrived. Then, too, accepting the child did not mean acknowledging paternity, which no one could believe anyway, since Tyverne had not been in England this past year, and he doubted if Miss Croft had been on the Peninsula.

Still, if he declared the child his, someone would have to bring a suit to refute the claim. Totty or Nonny could, if the infant were a boy, to avoid being cut out of the succession by a baseborn interloper. Ty could not imagine either of his brothers caring one way or the other who eventually took over the earldom. The earl would, though. Oh, how he would contest the claim. Ty could well envision his sire suffering a stroke at the thought of an outsider in line for his title. It might even be worth the aggravation to see the old man squirm with a bastard for a grandchild.

"Yes," he answered. "I am willing to accept the child. My debt to George Croft demands no less. I could not look at myself in the mirror otherwise."

Clarence was silenced, his wife was thinking about swooning again. Mindle was shaking his head, and Aunt Eliza's tears had changed to hiccups. Delia was staring at the viscount as if he'd just sprouted antlers.

The silence was broken by Dover, who skipped in, around the door. "Ain't those boots a treat, Major? Why, you can see yourself in 'em!"

Chapter 11

"Of all the arrogant, audacious . . ." Delia was so angry she could not think of the right words.

"Asinine?" Ty offered with a helpful half smile, wondering what he'd done to set the cat among the pigeons, this time.

"That, too." Delia grabbed the viscount's sleeve, to tug him from the room. She told the others, "You will excuse us, I am sure. Lord Tyverne and I obviously have a few matters to discuss in private."

"Private? Here, here, not at all the thing, is it, Gwen?"

"I'll make sure Cook packs up the rest of those ginger biscuits for you," Delia told her cousin.

"Well, I suppose that's all right, then." He leaped off the sofa, out of his wife's reach. "Ouch. Dash it, Gwen, I am going to be black-and-blue by tomorrow. What's that? Oh, yes, I am head of the household now, Dilly. You cannot be making these decisions by yourself, you know. I am the one to look after the welfare of the family, eh?"

"If you"—she glared at Clarence, then Tyverne—"either of you, cared one whit about my welfare or well-being, you would consult my wishes, not ride roughshod over them. I am neither a child nor a simpleton, needing your supervision."

"But, Dilly, my girl, you are a mere female. How can you know what's best?"

Ty might be a rough soldier, but at least he knew not to say *that* to a woman. He would not be surprised if Dilly—Delia—was the one to toss down the gauntlet to Sir Clarence. In fact, he decided to get her out of the room before she picked up a weapon. She was too near the fireplace poker, and Lud knew which of them she'd use it on first.

Delia was so angry that, in another minute, she feared, she would be throwing Clarence out of his own house. She needed to stay on at Faircroft a short while longer, which meant she needed to stay out of the nodcock's presence. As for the lummox who had her hand in his big paw again, well, she'd put a flea in his ear and send him on his way. If the officer was too ill to ride, he could take the family carriage with Clarence and Gwen, and take it back to Gwen's father's house, for all Delia cared. That way no one could malign her reputation, and she would have one less nuisance to deal with. She pulled him toward the door.

The problem was, where could she take the meddlesome major to give him a piece of her mind? Not his nearby bedroom, certainly, nor any of the other rooms on this floor where her cousins were sure to hear every word, if they had to stand with their ears against the walls. Below stairs the staff would be an equally attentive audience. Not outside or to the stables, for the bufflehead had left his boots behind. That left the master suite sitting room, the one Gwen coveted, so Delia led the viscount up the narrow winding staircase. She supposed she ought to have warned him about the low ceiling at the landing.

Before she could corral the angry words stampeding in her head, his lordship started to speak, to beg her pardon. His stiffly pronounced words barely penetrated her fury. He stood erect in the center of the room, a handsome, broad-shouldered statue, one that could have been titled *British Heroism* or *The Empire's Ares*. He was so strong, so sure of himself, never doubting his own authority or his own judgment, that Delia would have screamed her interruption, if she had not noticed him swaying on his feet.

"I beg your pardon, Miss Croft," he repeated to her back this time, for Delia had gone over to the drinks tray by the window. "I overstepped myself."

"No, what you did was ride in here with the intentions of examining the goods, making your offer, signing a few papers, then going on about your business, as if you were purchasing a horse instead of proposing marriage. You thought you could meddle in affairs that do not concern you, simply because you are used to being in charge, dash it."

The major took a deep breath. "You are correct. I should not have tried to force your hand that way, but I did truly believe I was acting in your best interests. I still feel that our marriage could be beneficial to both of us, if you would have me."

Delia practically slammed a glass of sherry into his hand. "Here, my lord, and sit down before you fall down." She kept another one for herself. Heaven knew she could use something to steady her nerves after shouting like a fishwife at the unfortunate featherhead!

The viscount took the glass as if it were a lifeline thrown to a drowning man and rubbed his head, looking around the elegant cream and gold room, with its gilded, spindle-legged chairs. Oddly enough, Delia thought, the officer did not look entirely out of place here, despite one button of his uniform being unfastened. She nodded toward a backless chaise. "That should not collapse under you."

Naturally he could not sit until she did, so Delia muttered, "Botheration," and threw herself into a cane-backed seat.

Tyverne swallowed half the thimble-sized glass of wine at once, then asked, "Is 'botheration' the only answer I am to get to my latest proposal? I rather thought a woman was supposed to thank the poor chap for the honor of his offer."

Delia drank her own sherry almost as hurriedly. "You, sir, are a gudgeon."

He nodded his agreement. He was here, wasn't he? "But other than that, I do not think I would be considered such a bad bargain on the London Marriage Market." He could not hide the shudder that swept through him at the thought. Delia got up and put another log on the fire.

"I mean," the viscount went on, "that aside from a few scars and this plaguey fever, I have all my teeth, my hearing, and my hair." He ran his fingers through his blond hair, wondering if he'd remembered to comb it. "And a hard head," he added, "to say nothing of the title, connections, and enough income of my own to support a household, with or without my father's largesse. When he dies . . . Well, that is in the future. Meanwhile, I can offer a woman my protection and my respect. I am neither clutch-fisted, a drunkard, nor a gambler. I seldom lose my temper, and have never raised my hand to a woman." Of course no woman had ever raised the temptation like this one, but Ty did not mention that fact. "I never would."

Delia was pacing now, too upset to sit still. "Next I suppose you will be telling me what an accommodating husband you would make, turning a blind eye to your wife's discreet liaisons, while you were free to conduct your affairs."

The viscount finished the contents of his glass. The thought of an unfaithful wife was enough to make a tippler out of him, after all. A wife was bad enough, but a wife who cuckolded him at every turn? Or, worst, presented him with yet another bastard to raise? He set the empty glass down before the crystal shattered in his grip. "Why, no. I expect my wife to honor her vows, the same as I expect from myself. I am not a libertine or a philanderer, Miss Croft."

"Well, a faithful husband is much to be desired, although a rarity these days, I understand. So that is something, I suppose."

"Something, but not enough?"

Oh, how Delia wished it were. Major Lord Tyverne seemed a decent sort. Stiff and reserved, and a prime example of a domineering male, but the glimpse of a smile she'd caught earlier proved the man could unbend occasionally. And he was devilishly handsome, smiling or serious. Marrying him would solve so many of her problems, and Aunt Eliza's, and her other dependents'. But then she, and all of them, would belong to this man who commanded armies. Delia would be another bit of what the Roman legions called *impedimenta,* the stuff they toted around with them. Or left behind when circumstances and the tides of war changed. Drat him, she thought. Drat the noble gentleman and his nobler offer, for tempting her to give up her dreams. She angrily shook her head, ignoring the hair that had come out of her braided coil. So what if she looked like she'd been dragged through a hedge backward? That was how she felt, by all that was holy! "No, I am sorry, my lord. It is not enough. It is not nearly enough."

Ty got up and poured himself another glass of wine. What he wanted to do was swill down the entire contents of the decanter, but he was not raised in the barracks, not entirely anyway. He refilled Miss Croft's glass, too, as she passed nearby in her pacing. She needed him, dash it! Why could she not see that? He could vanquish a hundred enemies, win a score of battles, wield an arsenal of weapons, yet he could not make one slim female yield to his reason and logic. "Devil take it," he cursed, forgetting he was not alone in his tent somewhere, "I don't know how to talk to a woman!"

Delia tilted her head to the side. "Excuse me?"

Flushing at his latest blunder, Ty decided he might as well explain. He sighed and said, "I knew I'd make a mull of things. You must have guessed by now I am not familiar with the gentler sex. I simply do not know the words you want to hear."

Unfamiliar with females, this blue-eyed Adonis? Delia would believe that when she saw pigs fly. Why, whenever he entered a room, women must throw themselves at his feet. His bare feet. She tore her eyes away from those naked digits, but her gaze unfortunately alighted on the vee at his neck, where neither his uniform coat nor his nightshirt was tightly fastened. She could see bronzed skin and the beginnings of golden chest hairs and— She walked back to the window, away from the hearth and its heat, to cool her cheeks.

"You want to know what I wish to hear?" she asked, and he nodded. "From the man I would marry, I want to hear words of love."

Ty was afraid of that. He shook his head. "I do not know them."

"Of course not," she explained, as if to a child. "You do not feel them."

"How could I feel them? That is, I do not know you. I do find you attractive and . . . and full of pluck."

"Thank you, I think. But you do not love me."

Ty wished he could undo another button. Lud, he had not had such an uncomfortable conversation since the colonel's wife wandered into his tent by mistake. He'd always hoped it was a mistake, at any rate. "I, ah, just met you yesterday" was all he could think to say.

"Exactly!" Delia was relieved she'd finally made this doggedly determined dolt see reason.

"You mean, in time . . . ?"

She stomped her foot—not even close to his lordship's toes, unfortunately—and said, "I mean, once and for all, that I want to marry a man who loves me. Me, not his own sense of honor. I want a man who wants me for myself, not because he feels duty-bound to wed, to fulfill his debts or obligations."

He started to speak, most likely to chide her for her childish imaginings, for believing in a happily ever after. She held up her hand. "Nay, let me finish, my lord. Your proposal was well-intended and well-spoken, and for that I do thank you. But even if I were willing to make an advantageous match without affection, which I am not, I would not wed a soldier."

"A rough breed, true, for a lady such as yourself, but—"

"But nothing. A soldier's code is God, King, and Country. Well, I wish to be first with my husband, not so far down the list as to be an afterthought! God, King, and Country," she repeated, making the words sound like a curse. "But what about family, I want to know? What about those depending on you to be here when needed?"

"The homeland needs to be defended."

"Of course," she bitterly replied. "That is what George said, that he was leaving home in order to protect it. There will always be that conflict between love and duty, and duty comes first, does it not?"

"Would you ask a man to forsake his honor?"

"Where is the honor in dying in some Godforsaken country, I ask you? You say you are not a gambler, yet a soldier gambles with his life in every battle. War is for fools, brave and proud fools—and their widows. I will never marry a soldier."

Now Ty understood why the generals did not accept married officers: their wives wrote letters. He thought of telling Miss Croft that he would most likely sell out, now that he could not serve in the field, but he would not lie. If his country called him, he would go, half-useless arm or not. It was as simple as that.

Nothing was as simple as that. "What about your child?"

"My child? What child?"

"The one you wrote George about, the one you were sewing tiny garments for, the one Nanny keeps praying for, and old Mags frets over. That child."

"You believe it is my child?" She sat down now, staggered. "And that is why you came? You offered for me, thinking I had a . . . a . . ."

"A love child," Ty supplied, although he doubted it was any such thing. The father was a soldier, he'd wager, to cause Miss Croft to despise the calling, some dastard who'd led her down the garden path, then abandoned her when his leave was over.

"You believed me a light skirt?" Delia looked daggers at him. "How dare you!" Then she had another thought: "And you would take me as your wife anyway? You are an even bigger fool than I imagined."

Ty was beginning to see the magnitude of his idiocy himself. He wished he had not given her that letter from her brother, so he could reread it. There was no time to ask to borrow the blasted thing, for Miss Croft was on her feet again and pulling him to his, toward a connecting door.

"Well, perhaps we can all be satisfied after all, my lord major," she said as they reached the door. "You are so eager to wed, and so anxious to repay your debt to my brother at any cost, while Lud knows poor Belinda desperately needs rescuing. It is a perfect match, I'd say. You might even call it a match made in Heaven."

She choked back a sob and threw open the door. "Here, sir, here is the legacy my brave and honorable brother George left us when he went to play at soldier. Here is the woman you meant to marry—and the child you offered to accept."

Chapter 12

The room was dark, the windows covered. At first, all Ty could discern was the old woman, Nanny, reading her Bible by the light of a candle. Then he saw a white cat on the heaped bedclothes. No, it was a small, scruffy dog, growling at the intruders, and the heap was not a pile of blankets and sheets at all. It was an immensely pregnant woman. He recognized the moaning now as she made a low keening sound without looking up.

"This, my lord, is Miss Belinda Gannon, my brother's betrothed," Delia whispered next to him, in the doorway.

My word, Ty thought. A proposal was bad enough, a marriage worse, but a lying-in? For all his heroism in battle, he would have fled this bedroom, but Miss Croft was blocking the doorway. "Is she . . . is she in labor?"

"She is in a comatose state, the physicians say. Sometimes she wakes and recognizes us. Most of the time, not. They have given up."

Delia stepped closer, petting the dog to quiet it, and then lit another candle. She beckoned Tyverne nearer the bed. With leaden feet, he inched forward. Belinda had been a beauty, he could see, with a heart-shaped face and long golden hair. To say she was deathly pale, however, was to overstate the case. Ty had seen that near-bloodless waxiness too many times not to recognize how tenuous a thread connected Miss Gannon to this earth. As he looked closer, he could see that her hands

by her side were swollen, the fingers bloated and tinged
with blue. He shook his head.

Delia was gently smoothing a lock of hair back from
Belinda's cheek. "Wake up, dearest, and see who has
come to visit. Lord Tyverne is a friend of George's from
the army."

Perhaps it was the sound of her beloved's name, but
Belinda did open her eyes. She saw a scarlet coat and
let out a glad cry. "George, you came back." She struggled to raise her arm from the top of the covers, holding
it out to him.

Ty had to take her cold hand in his. Once he had it,
he did not know what to do with the chill, limp burden.
He awkwardly patted it. "No, I am sorry. I am Tyverne,
but . . . but George sent me to . . . to look after you."

The girl moved her head from side to side, no longer
looking at him, or at anything of the real world. "Not
George. George is not coming home." She began that
low moaning again.

"I am so sorry, Miss Gannon." He carefully placed
her cold hand back at her side, atop the covers. "So
very sorry."

Nanny came to the other side of the bed and held a
glass to Belinda's mouth. The liquid dribbled out, onto
the girl's chin. "I doubt she can hear you anymore, milord, nor wants to, you not being Master George and
all."

And all. Did Belinda know that George had died saving Ty's life? Lud, could he feel more useless, more that
he never should have survived at the cost of young
Croft? Ty stared helplessly at the still form, knowing he
would hear those moans in his nightmares for the rest
of his life.

"Come," Delia said, touching his arm.

She poured Lord Tyverne and herself brandies this
time, from another decanter in the sitting room.

Ty stared out the window, reassuring himself that it
was still day, although he felt as if hours had passed since

he'd left this room. His skin was damp against his clothes, but his eyes and mouth felt dry and filled with grit, as if he'd ridden through a dust storm. He swirled the brandy around on his tongue, ignoring the stinging where he'd bitten his lip. He finally spoke: "She has such poor handwriting."

Delia was incredulous. "The poor girl is near death, her child with her. She has been forced from her home, and the man she loved is dead—and you find fault with her penmanship?"

"No, not that," Ty said, without turning from the window. He could not bear to see condemnation from yet another pair of eyes. "There was another letter in your brother's saddlebags, you see. One I could not decipher. If I had been able to—"

"You would never have offered for an antidote like me," Delia finished for him.

An antidote? Didn't George's sister know she had more beauty than twenty blond-haired, blue-eyed china shepherdesses? Now that he comprehended the difficulties she was facing, he understood her worried, ashen weariness. He admired her all the more for it, for shouldering such a burden. "No, I never would have importuned you with unwanted, unwarranted attentions. I would not have suspected you of—that is, I would have approached Miss Gannon, is it? To think, if her letter had been legible, I would have offered for her."

"It is not too late. You can still repay your debt to George by marrying his lover, and giving his bastard your name." Delia used the crude terms on purpose, not to sugarcoat the truth.

"Is she near to term, then?"

"She is nearer to death, by Mags's calculations, barring a miracle. That is Nanny's mission. Not trusting to Nanny's prayers, I had physicians from London come, and an expensive accoucheur, too. They held out no hope. One said Belinda had lost her will to live when George left. Another told me the child was evil, because of George and Belinda's immorality, and was poisoning her.

A third claimed the infant was lying wrong, blocking Belinda's vital humors."

Ty clutched at that. "Can the infant be turned? Sometimes they can, when mares or cows are struggling."

"He tried. Mags says he did more damage than good. I trust her judgment more than that of all the so-called learned men, for she's birthed nearly every child for miles. She says Belinda is too weak to go through labor now anyway, from neither eating nor drinking." Delia took a sip of the brandy and looked at the tall gentleman who was so noble he was actually considering her mad suggestion. "You would not long be burdened with an unwanted wife, therefore, nor have to claim the child as your own. But Belinda would not lie in a sinner's grave."

"Tell me," Ty said. "Tell me the rest of it, why they never married."

So Delia did. She spoke forever, it seemed to her, relieved to be placing more of her grief and anger and confusion on the viscount's broad shoulders. His gallantry no longer seemed so quixotic, as he listened patiently to her tell a tale that could rival *Romeo and Juliet* for tragedy—and childish stupidity.

Belinda Gannon and George Croft had been childhood playmates, it seemed, then sweethearts. They had always intended to be married. Her father, the local squire and major landowner after Lord Dallsworth, had smiled indulgently on the young couple until, that is, Belinda turned seventeen. Suddenly Squire's duckling was a swan. No longer an awkward, spotty girl, Belinda had turned into a beauty.

As she told the story, Delia tried to keep her own jealousy from coloring the narrative. She had always loved Belinda as a sister, expecting her to become one, in fact, eventually, but could never help feeling envious of the closeness the younger children shared. Then the squire's lumpish daughter turned out to be a Diamond. Delia, who began life as a scrawny girl with unkempt, unfortunately red hair and freckles, turned into a scrawny young lady with freckles, who had learned to keep her hair tamed in braids. None of the local boys would look at Delia, not when Belinda was nearby. Luckily for their friendship, Belinda had eyes only for George.

Squire was no longer amused. He thought he could do better for his only child than a mere country baronet with modest income and minor holdings. With her beauty, and a distant cousin's backing, Belinda could have a London Season next year, and reach as high as she wished on the matrimonial ladder.

Ignoring Belinda's pleas, Squire told her she was too inexperienced to know her own mind, that she should not settle for the first likely lad to bring her a posy. Ignoring George's entreaties, he told Delia's brother that he was too young, that George needed to sow a few wild oats now, to make sure he was not tempted, later. He refused permission for George to court Belinda, and then refused him permission to call at the cousin's house in London. His chick had to spread her wings, he said, without a cockerel hovering nearby.

So George decided to prove himself. He'd join the army while Belinda was off dancing and partying. He'd come back a hero, a man irrefutably, and claim the hand of his own true love.

Belinda had other ideas. She reasoned that if she was with child, her father would have to relent. George, naturally, was easily swayed to her thinking. Despite their best and enthusiastic efforts, it seemed, Belinda did not conceive.

The London Season and Belinda's departure date was growing closer, and Squire's impatience with George's presence on his doorstep was simply growing. Before he came to blows with his future father-in-law, the young baronet bought his commission and left for the Peninsula.

Not long after that, of course, Belinda found herself in an interesting condition. Her father did not find it quite as interesting when she returned to Kent before making her curtsies to the queen. Belinda gaily assumed her sire would now be happy to send her to join George and his regiment, so they could be wed before the baby arrived.

"What?" Ty interrupted. "Of all the corkbrained schemes, sending a young girl, in a delicate state besides, to follow the drum? Squire Gannon would have to be insane."

"He was, with anger."

Delia went on with the story: Squire was so angry, in fact, that he crossed Belinda's name out of his family Bible and threw his only daughter out of his house. He tossed her traveling bag and her little dog, which George had bought for Belinda, out with her. Nothing else did he let her take. Not coach fare, not her jewelry, not a memento of her dead mother's, not a shilling, not even a loaf of bread.

"He was the bastard," Ty muttered, then signaled that he was done interrupting.

Belinda came to Faircroft, of course. And Delia took her in, of course. They hid the pregnancy easily enough while they made plans, telling the neighbors that Belinda had come home to keep her betrothed's sister company.

Delia was going to accompany Belinda to the Peninsula and stay until the child was born, or until George could bring them all home. Aunt Eliza's nerves were too highly strung for her to accompany them, and Nanny was too old.

Delia had to stop talking here to take a sip of the brandy. The viscount was cursing too loudly for her to continue. "Two innocents in an army encampment, with nothing but a green lieutenant to look after them! That's going beyond lunacy to . . . to . . ." Ty could not think of anything to express his horror at the thought of what could have happened to the witless pair of young females.

"What was I supposed to do? I begged for Squire to accompany us. He refused. I pleaded with him to permit a marriage by proxy. He refused, and I could not get the thing done on my own, for Belinda is underage. I beseeched him to send us to a cottage somewhere, to wait for George, or the child. He refused. What would you have had me do?"

"You should have shot him. Go on. Finish the story."

They were nearly ready to leave when Belinda's pregnancy became difficult. She was ill all the time, and weakening. She became fretful, then fearful. How was Delia to get her into a carriage, much less onto a ship? She wrote again to George, and yet again, but the mails were uncertain, and the army was on the march.

Matters worsened, if possible, as the neighbors learned of Belinda's condition. Faircroft was censured, held up in church as a house of sin. Friends stopped calling, tradesmen stopped acknowledging the Croft accounts. In other, less enlightened times, Belinda—and Delia with her, tarred by the same brush—would have been stoned from the city gates. Now they were shunned.

And Clarence was in charge of the estate finances. He was horrified to have a fallen woman dropping her seed on his family tree and wanted nothing to do with Belinda. He would not let Delia withdraw more funds. She used her quarterly allowance, plus every groat she could squeeze out of the household accounts, thinning the staff, doing without, to afford the highly priced doctors.

Delia begged her own connections for help, but Aunt Rosalie was Clarence's aunt, too, and equally as miserly. She sent five pounds, as though that could find them a safe haven.

By then, it was horribly obvious that something was desperately wrong, and equally as obvious that Belinda had not counted her days correctly.

And then the letter came from the War Department, and it was too late altogether.

Clarence agreed to let Belinda stay on for her confinement, knowing it would not be long, one way or the other. He had little choice, since the army was slow to send George's effects home, and there might have been a will in his papers, leaving Belinda whatever was not entailed. Besides, Delia threatened to spread the rumor that Belinda's child was Clarence's if he did not let her stay.

She knew that was wrong, Delia confessed, but it was Faircroft or the poor house for Belinda—and for George's child. No one would have believed the rumor anyway, but Clarence lived in fear of scandal, so agreed.

Belinda had given up with George's death, and now Delia was forced to be more concerned about Belinda's eternity than her immediate future. The local vicar preached that what George and Belinda did was a sin, and she would go to Hell, without a stop in the hallowed graveyard. Clarence refused to consider burying her next to George in the Croft cemetery, and her father washed his hands of the whole matter. He would not come to encourage Belinda to get well, to eat for the child's sake. He would not come ease her mind with his forgiveness. He wished them both to the devil, instead, Delia concluded.

"But if you were to marry her," she told Tyverne, "then at least you could make sure Belinda has a place to rest. Her greatest sin was loving my brother, nothing more. Will you pay the debt you say you owe to George? Will you wed his bride?"

Chapter 13

Romeo and Juliet, hell, Ty thought. This was *Hamlet.* To be or not to be, wed, that is. As Miss Croft told Belinda's story, Ty listened, sipped his brandy, and pondered. His first conclusion was that life in the military was simpler, with the generals giving the orders, and the junior officers carrying them out. There were choices to be sure, life-and-death decisions, but they were often instinctual, instant, or decided on the basis of solid information. Here Ty was standing in quicksand. He did not even know if such a marriage would be legal, if the bride were not in her right mind. Likely not, but who would contest it?

His father, if Belinda lived. An earl's son marrying a baronet's sister was bad enough. Marrying a mere squire's daughter was worse. Taking to wife a squire's daughter no better than she ought to be was the worst choice yet—except for the prostitute his brother Nonny wanted to wed. Ty could not be sanguine about the scandalbroth either marriage would pour over the family name.

If, on the other hand, Miss Gannon did not survive the birth of her child, which unhappy outcome seemed likely, Ty would have the whole thing to do over, finding a woman to bear his heirs. He'd have gained a breathing space, though, to decide about his future in the army or out of it. Not even Stivern could put pressure on him when he claimed a mourning period out of respect for Belinda.

The whole thing felt wrong to Ty, unclean, somehow: wedding a woman who could not say nay, planning for after Belinda's death while she still breathed in the next room, wishing it was Miss Croft who needed him and his name instead.

The woman at his side was the woman the viscount would have married without hesitation. He'd been getting used to the idea, used to Miss Croft's inquisitive, intelligent nature and the way her red braided coronet caught the candlelight like a glowing halo. He had actually begun to look forward to learning her ways, learning her tastes, and what she tasted like. They might argue— Zeus, they would argue—but life with Miss Croft would not be boring.

The woman who lay so still in the other room, however, was the one George had left behind. She was also the woman whose child he had sworn to accept as his.

And Delia would never espouse a solider.

"Yes," Ty finally said. "I will wed Miss Gannon to serve George's memory."

Delia was almost disappointed, although she had expected nothing less. She already knew Lord Tyverne was a man of honor, although his skull was as thick as stone. His sense of duty could overcome any doubts he had, and his steady strength could see him through any difficulties. She did not mean the viscount's muscles and sinews, which were considerable, but his inner sureness. Here was an admirable man a woman could lean on . . . until he heard a higher calling.

Delia stifled the pang of regret she was feeling. This was what she wanted, wasn't it? A man to make an honest woman out of Belinda, to care for her, to make the choices Delia simply could not, or could not afford. Then why was she so disheartened by his decision She gave herself a mental shake. "Soon? Will the wedding be soon?"

Ty nodded. They both understood the unspoken need for haste. "Tomorrow. My man Winsted cannot have left Canterbury yet, so if you can find a fast messenger, my letter should reach him. He can exchange one special license for another, with the correct names." The viscount pulled an official-looking document out of his pocket. "The archbishop's secretary was not pleased with this one anyway, since he had to leave your name half blank. I could not have him write Dilly, and I knew none other for you."

While she searched out ink and pen and paper in the sitting room, Delia told him, "I never minded Dilly. Not terribly, anyway."

"I minded. Especially after meeting you. You are not silly or flighty as the name suggests, but you are more dignified, more a woman than a girl." And now he had no right to insist on or use either name.

Delia could not quite determine if he was giving her a compliment or labeling her a starchy old spinster. She decided his opinion of her no longer mattered, if it ever did. "Are you sure the archbishop will agree?"

"After the donation I made, above the fee? I should think so. He knows the story, or as much as I knew. He and my father have had their differences, too, so he will do it, knowing how much the earl would be opposed."

"Displeasing your father does not bother you?"

"I have never pleased my father, and will not start living my life to try now." He sharpened the pen she handed him and started to write. "I'll have Winsted fetch Stephen Anselm back with him, too, to perform the ceremony. He's a vicar on the archbishop's staff. From what you said, I find your local vicar to be singularly lacking in Christian charity. Not the sort I'd want at the wedding."

"But you know this Reverend Anselm? He'll come?"

"We went to university together, and pulled each other's chestnuts out of the fire countless times. I've found staff positions for any number of young cubs he wanted looked after, and wrote checks for his pet charities. Anselm will demand a new roof for some church or other, but he will come if I ask."

Delia took up another sheet of paper and a pencil, to make a list of what needed to be done if the ceremony was to be the very next day. "Shall I invite Belinda's father?" she asked.

"The man who would let his daughter fall by the way-side? I think not." He went back to writing his letter to Winsted, his former batman.

Delia interrupted again. "What about Clarence and Gwen? Shall I ask them to attend?"

"It is your home, Miss Croft, or Croft's, but they are your relations, neither mine nor Miss Gannon's—my, ah, my future wife's." Ty nearly reverted to stammering at the dreadful phrase, but he got it out. "You must do as you see fit, of course, but I doubt Sir Clarence will accept."

Not witness a viscount's nuptials in his own house? Delia could not imagine Clarence forsaking such a heady treat, much less the wedding breakfast, subdued though it must be. Gwen would never let him. The wedding at Faircroft could only strengthen her position in the local society, and give her yet another opportunity to flaunt her finery. "He will come."

Ty did not bother looking up. "Not after I give him my opinion of his treatment of the gentlewomen in his care."

Delia flashed him a smile. Large military gentlemen had their uses, after all. "But whom shall you have to stand up with you, your batman?"

"Possibly, if he's brought his dress uniform into Kent with him. We were not expecting to stop here for long. Sergeant Winsted is more an aide-de-camp than a valet. He and I have been through a lot together, though, so perhaps it would be fitting. Otherwise Mindle can be groomsman, if he will. I daresay he has more refinement than either of us army chaps. Oh, and I think we should have a solicitor present. Do you have one you can call on?"

"Clarence has been consulting Mr. Hedgewick, in Dover, about George's estate, I believe."

"No, that won't do. Not that I distrust Hedgewick, but I would rather have a different man, not connected to your cousin. Anselm will know an honest fellow to bring as witness, to ensure the legalities."

Delia was counting how many people she would have to offer refreshments, if not accommodations. Would they arrive in time for breakfast tomorrow? Stay for supper? She had to be prepared. Her own list was growing, with barely an afternoon and evening to accomplish everything.

"Is there anything else I am forgetting?" Tyverne asked, before he sealed his letter for the waiting messenger.

"What about a ring? I have one I could give you for Belinda but—" But it was a family heirloom. Somehow Delia did not think the viscount would be happy marrying George's bride in George's house using George's mother's ring.

"No, thank you. I purchased one when I was in London. I had no idea of your—that is, the size, or what style you—ah, Miss Gannon would prefer. The St. Ives wedding set is in the vault in Warwickshire." Where his father would guard it from unworthy daughters-in-law like a dragon guarding its horde of gems.

He showed her a plain band, solid and respectable, like Viscount Tyverne himself. The polished gold even gleamed like the highlights of his hair. Delia sighed and went back to her lists. "We should have flowers."

"Flowers," he repeated. "Every wedding has at least a few blooms, doesn't it? This time of year might make obtaining them difficult, but Winsted is used to foraging. Belinda deserves flowers for her wedding, don't you think?"

Delia was beginning to think that, if Belinda recovered, the poor little widgeon was getting far more than any girl deserved.

*   *   *

Ty felt better when he was planning the event than he did thinking of the event. It was the same as a campaign: figuring the logistics was engrossing, predicting the enemy's actions, preparing for every eventuality from ambush to damp ammunition. Fighting the actual engagement was nearly mechanical, like an actor in a well-rehearsed role. It was in the space between, when a man had time to think, that doubts and desperation festered. Like now.

Ty had taken care of as many details as he could this afternoon, directing his minions, authorizing payments, giving orders half of which, he suspected, Miss Croft would ignore or countermand. Tomorrow, at the actual ceremony, with Winsted and Anselm at his side, he knew he would stand firm. He had never turned his back on a battle yet. This evening, however, alone in his room, Major Lord Tyverne was quaking. He kept feeling his forehead for fever. No such luck.

He was getting married, to a woman. Well, of course he was wedding a woman, Ty acknowledged, but, Jupiter, he was actually getting leg-shackled. To a female. His mind suffered a paroxysm at the notion.

Then he recalled that he was growing more at ease around the gentler sex. Not that Miss Croft was so delicate, giving him a rare trimming, despite his apology, for believing her a straw damsel at first. She was right; Ty should not have leaped to conclusions. Then she'd stuck to her guns about him not moving to the inn for the night to protect what was left of her reputation. She did not back down, not even when he used his best parade-ground command voice. And she was right again, dash it. Ty doubted if he could have mounted, much less ridden Diablo to the inn, his legs were so unsteady. Either way, he seemed to be getting used to Miss Croft's company. He hardly chewed on his lip when conversing with her anymore, and had not broken out in a sweat once while they made plans. He'd even made her smile again, when he suggested Dover as ring bearer.

If he could overcome his misgivings about Miss Croft, Ty thought, surely he could manage to marry Belinda . . .

a sickly, pregnant young female who loved another man so much she was dying of a broken heart.

Lud.

Lord Tyverne had relieved half of his anxiety by frightening Sir Clarence half to death. The baronet would not attend the wedding. Neither would he mention taking possession of the house until Belinda, the future Viscountess Tyverne, could be safely moved. Ty choked off the baronet's complaints—and just a bit of the baronet's breathing—before he offered to reimburse the clunch for provisions, servants' salaries, stabling for the horse, and whatever else the nip cheese could think of. As for browbeating his cousin into accepting Lord Dallsworth, now that Miss Croft was not marrying the viscount, well, Clarence would not do that, either. Not if he wished to show his face in London, Kent, or Warwickshire, or half the counties between, to say nothing of Spain and Portugal.

Ty still had the night to get through. He tried to sleep, but his mind kept returning to the morrow, to the wedding that would be stranger than any he could have imagined. When he commanded his brain to picture other, less nerve-racking scenarios, like a firing squad, he saw only Delia, Miss Croft—naked, with her red hair loose around her shoulders. No, the major would not be getting much sleep this night. He put on his boots.

The house was quiet, for once devoid of the sounds of sorrow. Mindle and Dover were in the kitchens, he knew, helping with the cooking and polishing; Miss Croft and the other women were above, doing whatever females did to prepare for a wedding. Men prepared by going out with friends, gambling, drinking, whoring.

Ty went to the stables to share a bottle of ale with his horse.

Chapter 14

*B*elinda's room looked like a bower, with sun coming through the opened curtains. Delia had brought potted palms and ferns from all over the house, and found some ivy that had stayed green. The efficient Winsted had brought early violets from a flower seller in Canterbury, and roses from someone's succession houses. There was also a large arrangement on the dressing table that looked suspiciously like an altar piece. The bedchamber smelled like a garden now, though, instead of a sickroom.

After conferring with Lord Tyverne, Delia had decided against disturbing Belinda by moving her to the master suite sitting room or, heaven help them, the formal parlor. Trying to wrestle the unresponsive, unwieldly bulk down those narrow stairs would have been hazardous for all of them. Instead, they had dressed poor Belinda in a pretty pink robe of Delia's, with a fall of lace added to the front so no one would notice it did not close. Delia and Aunt Eliza had added more lace to the cuffs, to cover the girl's bloated hands and wrists. They'd washed and dried her hair, fanning it across the pillow in a golden sweep, and placed a garland of pink roses atop her head. They spread a lacy white gauze cover over her blankets, almost like a wedding veil, and scattered a few rose petals on top of it. The dog, who had been washed and dried and combed also, had a ribbon around its neck. Delia patted the little terrier to keep it from barking at all the strangers, then placed a single pink rose by her friend's side.

Belinda could have been a sleeping princess from a fairy tale waiting for her handsome prince—except for the immense mound of her belly. Those bewitched beauties were seldom breeding. Then, too, they were rarely whiter than their sheets, nor did make-believe brides have blue-tinged lips and labored breathing.

Still, Delia thought as she took her place near the bed, Belinda was getting married. Tyverne might not be Belinda's first choice of husband, nor was he a prince in fact or fancy—not with his serious, gruff manner and bellowing voice—but he made a handsome groom, shining from his fair curls to his gold buttons to his black leather boots. More importantly, he was a good man, stalwart and true to what he believed was right. That was far more crucial in a husband than a facile tongue or a ready smile, Delia decided, looking across the bed at the uniformed gentleman. Tyverne had substance, aside from his strength, and he would use it on Belinda's behalf.

He would know what to do for Belinda, be it better doctors or more medicines. She would have the best care in the world, not just what a handful of old women and one youngish old maid who knew nothing of birthing could provide. The infant—and here Delia sent a prayer skyward—would never want for anything, especially not a name. There would always be rumors and gossip, but Delia recalled what Ty had said about boys calling him Archy. He protected what was his.

Someday, perhaps, Delia hoped, she could find such a mate for herself. He did not have to be so large, of course, nor so handsome or highly stationed, not even as wealthy, simply as kind and decent. And he would love Delia unconditionally, freckles, red hair, skinny bosom and all, with his heart and soul, for this was her fairy tale.

Ty was standing at the opposite side of the bed from Miss Croft, between Mindle and Winsted, with the new solicitor, Macurdle, behind him. That was good, he thought, for they could catch him when he passed out. Stephen Anselm stood at the foot of the bed, grinning despite the solemnity of the occasion, at his friend's discomfort. Everyone else, including Winsted, assumed Ty's ashen color and trembling hand were due to the remnants of the fever. To the devil with old friends.

And with such folderol as this. The ceremony should have been over ages ago, if not for Stephen's babbling. The papers could have been signed, and he could have been on his way back to London, to see what new nonsense his brother Nonny was up to. If Anselm read one more verse of scripture, Ty might have to wait another day to make the journey, deuce take it.

The women seemed to be enjoying the ritual. Nanny, Aunt Eliza, and old Mags were arrayed beside Miss Croft on the other side of Belinda's bed, with Cook and two housemaids whispering and giggling for Stephen Anselm's attention behind them. They'd decorated the room to look like a pagan altar, and poor Miss Gannon to resemble the virgin sacrifice. Except for the infant, of course. Now they were lined up across from the males like the opposing camp, girded for battle with rose petals and Bibles. Lud, did they think he would retreat at this point? He might have, except for balding Macurdle behind him, and gap-toothed Dover between him and the door, the ring on a small pillow in the urchin's freshly scrubbed hands.

This was not a war. The women were not his enemy. Belinda was merely a foolish female who needed his help, a young girl who might have found herself in such extremities, even if George Croft had lived and come home. Finally, Ty told himself, a man's heart did not stop beating when he stepped into parson's mousetrap. That would have defeated the purpose of the whole endeavor.

He was not going to collapse, and he was not going to cast up his accounts—he hoped. To redirect his thoughts while Anselm droned on—the viscount would have a few words of his own, later, in regard to his friend's wordiness—with Nanny's prayers echoing in an undertone, Ty looked at Miss Croft.

She was pleasant to look at this morning, more so than usual. Her face had a little more color, although she still looked weary, as well she should, having accomplished so much in such a short time. Delia was wearing a lavender dress of half mourning for the occasion, a black ribbon threaded through the trim at the neckline and at the short sleeves. The color did not become her, Ty thought, not with her hair, but it was better than the moldy black she'd had on previously. She must have considered the colors to be clashing also, for she'd placed a lace cap over most of her red curls. If Ty had the dressing of her—or the undressing, God forgive him for the thought—the cap would be the first thing to go. He decided that she would look good in green to match her eyes, or amber, like the flecks that danced in them when she was angry or agitated, which seemed most of the time in his company. Today she was gazing at him with approval, perhaps even respect, for a change. No, he could not disgrace himself now, not in the face of her rare approbation. He would even manage to speak the marriage cows—the vows!—without stumbling.

Soon enough, that time came. Now, Ty thought, instead of going as slow as a snail, his old friend Anselm was speeding the thing along. Thunderation, Ty should have had the local vicar do the deed after all.

When directed, the viscount placed his gold ring in the palm of Belinda's ice-cold hand, trying without success to fold her swollen fingers around it. Holding it there with his own, almost as cold and uncooperative hand, he started to repeat after Anselm: "I, Archimedes—" He paused to glare at the maid who giggled again, and at Anselm, to remind him of a few black eyes and bloodied noses. "With this ring I, Archimedes Arthur Forrest St. Ives . . ."

He got through it, leaving out only one of his many given names.

Delia spoke for the bride: "Belinda Helen Gannon."

Aunt Eliza wept a little harder to hear Belinda's name, not her niece's.

But now the solicitor behind Ty began to shuffle his feet and clear his throat. The man had not been happy with the situation. He understood the necessity—Lud knew, he had daughters. But the details were what bothered him. He was a lawyer, after all.

"No one is going to contest the wedding," Ty had insisted.

"When I draw up a contract," Macurdle had replied, "no one bothers to try. That is why you chose to employ my services, is it not?"

The Reverend Mr. Anselm had found the best solicitor he could, thinking it would be just like Ty's father to try to set aside a marriage he had not sanctioned. No matter that the church approved, or the courts recognized the legality, the earl could look for a reason to have this union annulled. Refusing to consider that Miss Gannon might not survive, Ty's old friend was worried about any future children this couple he was joining together might produce. If he were able to prove the ceremony flawed, the earl could have the marriage declared null and void, which would make all of Tyverne's offspring illegitimate, not just this troublesome one. None of them would thus be able to succeed to the title. In effect, Stivern could disinherit Ty after all for not bending to his will.

The special license obviated the necessity for permission of a parent or guardian, Macurdle agreed. But he had been concerned with the matter of volition. "Otherwise, my lord, unscrupulous fortune hunters could kidnap heiresses to wed *nolo-volo,* will she or won't she, by means of a special license."

Macurdle tried to consult with Belinda himself, so he could swear she was entering into this binding contract of marriage of her own free will. Either she did not hear him, or she did not have the strength to answer. Or she simply did not care. Belinda was no longer making those sorrowful exhalations, which Ty and Delia tried to convince themselves meant she was not in pain. Unfortunately, she was making no sounds at all.

"Usually in cases such as this, a trustee speaks for the one who is incompetent to know his or her rights. That surrogate must ensure that the incapacitated subject's welfare is being duly considered." Macurdle looked around.

"I can speak for Belinda," Delia said. "She came to live with me when her father disowned her, so that should prove she trusts me."

"And today is proof of the depths of your devotion, to be sure," Mr. Macurdle replied, not meeting her eyes. "But you are, I am afraid, a mere young woman, incapable in the eyes of the law of making your own decisions, much less another, younger female's."

While Delia was brooding about being a mere anything, Ty suggested they get the local magistrate to come act as Belinda's watchdog. That was not an option, however, for Squire Gannon, Belinda's father, was the magistrate. He could not be considered unbiased nor to have a care for the girl's future. He'd likely appoint the village drunk to be Belinda's guardian if they brought the issue to his court.

As witness, the solicitor should not also represent one of the parties. As groom, Lord Tyverne should not speak for the bride.

They decided, therefore, that Stephen Anselm, the man of the cloth, adjunct to the archbishop himself, was the best person, and the least likeliest to have his decisions challenged, to represent Belinda's best interests. Reverend Anselm firmly believed that this marriage was fitting and proper under the eyes of the church and the laws of the land. And that the child should have a father. So the marriage had proceeded.

Now, however, they were at the I-do's part of the ceremony, and Belinda didn't. Macurdle cleared his throat once more. "I am sorely troubled by Miss Gannon's lack of a response."

Anselm was more troubled at the way the groom and

the bridesmaid were gazing at each other. He spoke louder: "Do you, Belinda, take Archimedes—"

"She does not know any Archimedes," Delia impatiently interrupted. "Let me try." She leaned over the bed and stroked Belinda's cheek. "Dearest, Tyverne is here again. Remember him? He was here yesterday. He wants to marry you, to take care of you and the baby. Please, Belinda, please tell him you would like that."

She got no response, so she added: "George sent him, remember?"

As before, the sound of her lover's name was the only thing to reach that place where Belinda waited. "G-george?"

Ty stepped forward so she could see his uniform. He could not lie, but he did not have to tell her the truth. He patted her hand, not knowing if Belinda could feel his touch. "You have to be strong, my dear, for me and the babe. Tell me now, do you want to be married?"

"Oh, I . . . do."

At least ten people sighed in relief. The vicar quickly concluded, and pronounced Ty and Belinda man and wife just as Belinda whispered, "That was all . . . I . . . ever wanted, Geo—"

Anselm almost shouted: "You may now kiss the bride."

Ty had already laid his fingers across Belinda's lips to keep George's name from issuing forth. Now he bent lower and touched his lips to her forehead.

"You . . . stay?"

Ty repeated the vow he had just made: " 'Til death do us part."

Chapter 15

M indle was ready with champagne in the sitting room, although no one was quite able to compose a suitable toast for the occasion. "To the health of the bride and groom" did not seem appropriate, nor did "to a fruitful union."

Ty raised his glass—his hands had stopped shaking as soon as he'd said the fateful words—and thanked the assembled company. He thanked the servants and Miss Croft and Delia's aunt, for their hard efforts. He thanked his friend Anselm and the solicitor for coming, and then he thanked everyone for their good wishes.

"To good wishes" rang out amid a flurry of hugs, back-slaps, and clinking glasses. And Aunt Eliza's happy sniffles, of course.

Delia came to congratulate the viscount without knowing if she should offer her hand or her cheek to show her gratitude and her admiration. Major Lord Tyverne might be a stiff-backed soldier, but he had been a good friend to George and Belinda, and Delia and he had worked well together making plans. She still had a glass in her hand, so she simply mouthed the fitting words, smiled, and waited.

There went Ty's composure. He'd been feeling much more in command now that the deed was done. Belinda was in Mags's capable hands, so he could get his breath back, then get on the road as soon as the papers were signed. Now here was Miss Croft, making splinters of his sangfroid, crumbs of his confidence, dross of his dignity. Hell, she was making mice feet of his manhood. Zeus, her smile tied a man in knots.

Just like a woman, though, Miss Croft created havoc, then stood there, waiting for him to do something, as if an army officer knew the first thing about drawing room manners. Was he to kiss her, as Aunt Eliza had insisted, or bow? The viscount knew what he wanted to do, but . . .

But the room was full of people, and worse, the unpredictable woman might take offense and slap him. Worst of all, Belinda lay in the next room, his brand-new wife. His wife, by all that was holy. Ty had a wife, and Miss Croft was not her. She. It.

Blast, he thought, one smile and he was a blithering fool—a blithering fool with impure thoughts, besides. The sooner he was on his way the better. He signaled Mindle to refill her glass. "Papers, that's it. Papers to sign, you know," he said as he fled.

The man had to be the coldest fish Delia had ever known. She sipped at her wine and watched as the viscount joined Anselm and Macurdle at a table with documents laid out on it. Not one friendly word could he speak, much less let his mouth turn up in a smile. He looked like he'd sucked on sour lemons, in fact. Delia could have kicked herself for her momentary lapse in common sense, wishing for an instant that things might have been different. Botheration, if things had been different, Belinda would be Lady George Croft, Major Lord Tyverne would be with his troops in the Peninsula, and Delia would still be the spinster sister with no home of her own.

Granted this was not the most auspicious of occasions, and not a true celebration, but Tyverne could have given her a pleasant nod, not just the thanks he had expressed to her—and the servants. After all, he had what he wanted, what he had come for. His honor was satisfied. She hoped his honor kept him warm at night; the ice-cold blood that ran through his glacier of a heart surely would not. She went to invite Mr. Anselm to take refreshments in the dining room.

The vicar was a charming, outgoing gentleman, not at all like his friend. He flirted with her, then with Aunt Eliza, complimenting the older lady's lace bonnet. Delia's aunt started to look more closely at the nicely spoken fellow, calculating that he was well connected, if he was friends with a viscount, and well positioned for advancement in the church. Best of all, he seemed well able to please a finicky female, to judge by Delia's laughter and the sparkle in her eye. Then he mentioned a vow of celibacy. Aunt Eliza needed a new handkerchief.

When Ty reached Macurdle's side, the solicitor was beaming, the second glass of wine in his hand. "That was a near thing, my lord, but I am pleased to affix my seal as witness. Not that I worried that a gentleman of your reputation would take part in anything underhanded, of course, but I am satisfied now. Anyone could see Miss Gannon was in no shape to respond, well, her shape alone, that is, should have been answer enough to the question. But the lady did speak."

Sergeant Winsted was still muttering about how they should have had the cheap lawyer when he affixed his signature to the marriage documents. They could have been halfway to London by now.

Ty was too busy to answer, wondering how he could ever have thought Stephen Anselm a decent chap. He left out a different middle name this time, when he signed.

Then Mr. Macurdle called to Miss Croft to add her signature. She never glanced at Tyverne when she was done, but invited all of the men to join her and her aunt at a wedding breakfast.

Ty did not see how he could refuse. The wedding was his, after all. But he was not hungry enough to stomach watching his best friend banter and laugh with Miss Croft, things he'd never be able to do, Ty was sure. Better to offend her now by leaving, than to sit mumchance at her table watching Anselm spread his charm around like butter. The man was a vicar, by Jupiter. And Ty was married.

He was about to make his excuses when old Mags came into the room from the connecting door. "You'd best come back in now, my lord," she told the viscount. "And you too, Miss Dilly. And the vicar."

They entered Belinda's room and could tell the difference immediately. They could all hear it, the rasping breaths coming too far apart.

Mr. Anselm knew. The vicar immediately went to the bedside and began praying, Nanny a low descant behind him.

Delia knew. She pulled a chair to the other side of the bed and held Belinda's hand. "Please, Belinda," she begged, "please, dearest, hold on awhile more, for George and the baby." But not a flicker appeared behind the blue-veined eyelids, not even at the mention of her beloved George.

Ty knew. He had seen Death so many times, in so many miserable ways, he had to know its face. But not like this. Not a woman. Not a pretty young lady still in her teens, not with her life ahead of her and a child to bring forth. No, this was not right, not an honest death fighting for what one believed in. This was an atrocity, an abomination. What had this poor girl done that was so bad to deserve such a fate? She had loved too much? Scores of other young lovers had loved too early, from all the eighth-month infants, and they never paid such a terrible price.

Ty shook his head, no. No, the awful injustice was too great to be born, and no, he would not stand by, helplessly watching. He could not. He'd leave his man Winsted here with a carte blanche to make whatever arrangements Delia wanted, but he would set off now, if he had to drive the coach himself.

"I . . ." he tried to explain. "London."

Delia looked up at him, still near the door. Tears were beginning to trail down her cheeks, but she tried to smile for him. "I know you would have taken her there to the best surgeons and physicians, or sent carriages for them to come. They would have, more than answered my messages. But it is too late, my lord. There is nothing more to be done except pray and make your farewells."

Delia held her other hand out to Ty as if she were offering him comfort, when she was the one who was bidding her best friend adieu so shortly after losing her brother. She was the one who was going to be alone in the world except for an old aunt to care for, Ty knew, and a chaw-bacon cousin who cared for naught but appearances. Miss Croft was losing a near-sister, her home, and her recent *raison d'etre,* but she was thinking of Belinda, not herself. His estimation of her character, of womanhood in general, rose in the face of such generosity. Ty had no choice but to go to her, to stand beside Delia's chair at the side of the bed, clasping her fingers.

Even the dog knew, whimpering and shivering at the foot of the bed until Ty started stroking its head with his free hand.

Aunt Eliza came in, clutching her wadded handkerchief. She tried to say something, but settled for kissing her fingertips, then touching them to Belinda's lips. Mindle came to lead her out, before she collapsed.

Now those breaths of Belinda's were more ragged, impossibly far apart.

Reverend Anselm finished reading from his prayer book and nodded toward Delia. She stood and leaned forward, her tears freely flowing. "I wish . . . I wish we had been sisters, Belinda, and I wish I could have held my niece or nephew, but I know you will be happier now, because you will be with George. Tell him I miss him, and our parents. Tell him . . . tell him that I love him, and I am glad he will not be alone. Good-bye, dearest Belinda. Go in peace."

Delia took the handkerchief Ty held out to her. Then she looked at him expectantly. Stephen Anselm nodded at his friend, then jerked his head more forcefully toward the dying woman.

Ty looked at her, this wife that he had never known,

the woman Lieutenant Croft had died trying to return to. Ty had tricked her into giving her consent to wed a stranger, then he had promised to stay with her, 'til death did them part, knowing he was leaving as soon as he could. He cleared his throat. "I am sorry I was the one to come home, my lady, not your George. And I am sorry I could not help you more. I am so very sorry."

"You must not blame yourself," Delia told him, wiping her eyes. "Events had progressed too far, long before you ever encountered my brother."

Ty shook his head. How could he not regret his part in this tragedy? He turned back to Belinda. "Tell George thank you. And tell him I tried, by Heaven. Farewell, Lady Tyverne."

Reverend Anselm placed his hand on Belinda's forehead and blessed her, saying, "Our daughter, Belinda Helen Gannon St. Ives, your Father forgives you of your sins. You are loved, my child. Go with God."

Delia turned her head away, onto the viscount's chest. Lord Tyverne was there, and he was strong and real and smelled of soap, not the flowers they had brought in to cover the sickroom odors. She could borrow his strength, his courage, just for a little while. He was a soldier, so surely he could comprehend the need to share one's grief with someone else who understood. For this moment she was not concerned that the officer could barely tolerate her presence, as long as he let her shelter in his arms.

Stunned, Ty could only react, not by fleeing, as he would ordinarily have done from a weeping woman, but by wrapping his arms around Miss Croft. Delia. He stroked her back, almost the same way he had comforted the dog, but not the same at all. Nothing in Ty's nine and twenty years had ever felt as right as holding this woman while she cried. Not that he was feeling glad she was grieving, just that she had turned to him. Hell, he did not know what he was feeling, did not have the words to describe it. He was a soldier, by Jupiter, not a poet.

Ty felt complete—that was it. Delia filled his arms perfectly, and fit precisely under his chin, her soft curves brushing against his chest. Not that this was a physical feeling, Ty swore to himself. Lud, what kind of cad would he be, to lust after a woman while her friend lay dying? Especially when her friend was his wife! No, that was not it at all, although under different circumstances . . .

The usually self-assured Delia trusted him enough to show her weaker side, like the dog turned on its back. She thought he was a rock to lean on, instead of the sponge-spined coward Ty knew he was with women. She thought he was strong. She was wrong, and the viscount knew he had to leave before she found out. She'd discover his failings as soon as he opened his tongue-tied mouth—but what was there to say anyway? Delia Croft would never marry a soldier. She wanted a gentleman, and deserved nothing less. Ty was not free to ask, no matter how good she felt in his embrace. Poor Belinda was not yet in her grave, and he owed her—and George—far more respect than to be sighing over another woman. He sighed anyway. The sooner he left, the better for all of them.

Delia was not done weeping, and Ty was not done convincing himself he had to take his arms away now. They might have stayed like that forever, except Mags scowled at them and said, "But what about the babe?"

Chapter 16

"*W*hat do you mean, what about the babe?" Ty almost shouted, forgetting where he was. Actually, he'd already forgotten where he was, but, oh, hell, one did not bellow at a deathbed. He dropped his arms from Miss Croft so fast she staggered, and he winced with the pain from his wounded arm at such sudden motion.

Belinda was still breathing, though barely, and old Mags had pulled the covers down to listen for a heartbeat. Then she moved her ear lower to that distended mass. "The infant's heart is still going steady. Not for long, for neither of them, I wager, but there is a chance for the wee one."

"But you said Belinda was not ready to give birth." Delia blew her nose and watched the midwife poke at the mound of Belinda's stomach.

"She will never be ready, not now. But we can make a way for the baby to come out. The Romans did it."

"The Romans also left unwanted children outside the gates for the wolves to eat," Ty said.

"Aye, but I have heard of a few other cases where it has been done," Mags replied. "I read of two such at Edinburgh, where they teach the physicians what little the rattle-pates know."

"Yes, but were any of them successful?" Ty wanted to know.

"Not for the mother, that's the truth. But sometimes

the infant survives. I don't see as we have much to lose, my lord."

Delia's face had drained of color. "You mean cut Belinda open, while she still lives? But that would be murder, would it not?"

Ty looked at Anselm, who shrugged. "I do not think Lady Tyverne's life is ours to give or take any longer, but the child's? That would be the miracle of birth, surely not a crime."

"Macurdle!" Ty bellowed in his officer's voice, loud enough to be heard above the roar of cannons. Belinda was past hearing, anyway.

The whole household, it seemed, appeared in an instant. The solicitor listened to what Ty asked, looked to the midwife with her sharp knife, and promptly slid to the floor in a dead faint. So much for the legal opinion. Winsted, who knew better than to ignore the major's command, directed at him or not, dragged the lawyer out of the room. Mindle and Aunt Eliza leaned on each other, both ashen and trembling.

"You'd better hurry and decide," Mags told the viscount. "Another minute and it will be no use."

They were all looking at him. Of course they were. He was the woman's husband, her lawful spouse, the one authorized by the church and the crown to make life-and-death decisions for her and the issue of her body. Lud, first he had held Miss Croft in his clumsy hands, now he held a child's life. He was not qualified for either.

"Likely the babe won't live anyway," Mags was saying. "And if it should, you've got even odds it'll be a girl, no threat to your title and all that nonsense men put such stock in. If it's a boy, the world will know he's a bastard no matter what you do, but at least he'd have a chance to live."

Delia was looking at him with hope for her brother's child.

Anselm had his eyes on Belinda, holding his own breath between her rattling respirations. "Hurry, Ty. Decide."

A long shot, Ty calculated, that was what the infant had. A chance. The same slim chance that George Croft had given a mortally wounded man in the midst of battle. "Live to pass on the favor." That's what the lieutenant had said as he sent Ty to safety on his horse. "Save someone else's life." Major Tyverne had not saved the lieutenant's sweetheart. He had to try for the babe.

He nodded. "Do it."

Mags and Nanny started to unwrap Belinda's covers and pile blankets and towels beside her. Delia sent Mindle for hot water, rags, brandy. Aunt Eliza huddled in a corner using the little dog in her arm as a towel.

"Wait!" Ty ordered. "This is no place for Miss Croft or her aunt. My man Winsted and I have seen more blood and gore than all of you combined. We will assist Mags. The rest of you, get out. Except for you, Anselm. And you, too, Nanny. You stand there and pray. Pray for all your soul is worth, for all of us."

Delia did not leave, of course. She made ready a clean basket, with the softest cloths and placed it to warm by the fire. When Winsted turned green at the first cut of the knife, though, she was there at Ty's side, following the midwife's instructions.

The room was so hot, for the baby, Mags said, that sweat poured off Ty's forehead. He took off his coat and tossed it aside. Hours seemed to pass while they listened for Mags's orders, Belinda's breaths, and Anselm's prayers. And then . . . and then there was a baby.

"Small," Mags declared, "but breathing."

She placed the infant on the waiting towels to cut and tie the cord, and the child made a noise, more like something a kitten would make than a baby, but it lived!

"A girl, my lord," Mags said, before handing the infant to Nanny for cleaning. They all smiled and started to cheer, until they noticed the vicar remove the garland of flowers from Belinda's hair and draw a sheet over her face.

"Plenty of time for that later," Mags said when Delia brushed a tear from her eye. "Go help Nanny with the babe now." She went back to the mother, making her ready for the grave.

The others returned to the sitting room, where the solicitor had revived and was having a drink. The men joined him, while Delia and Aunt Eliza rhapsodized over the infant as Nanny dressed her, near the hearth for warmth.

The newborn was hardly moving, and had not made so much as another mewl of protest at being torn from her warm, watery nest, not even when Nanny wrapped her tightly in soft flannel. The old nursery maid had not swaddled a babe since George had been born, but she remembered how, and showed Delia. Then she shook her head when she handed the tiny bundle to the infant's aunt by blood, if not by law.

"Methinks, Reverend, we'd best get this wee lass churched," the old woman called across the room, going back to the bedchamber to fetch her Bible. "The sooner the better, I'd say."

Ty went over to Delia, who was standing by the fireplace, rocking the infant in her arms. He looked over her shoulder at the new life she cradled.

The babe was as beautiful as a da Vinci cherub, if not as rounded or rosy-cheeked. Her hair was wet, but it looked pale and downy, with no reddish cast at all, Ty was pleased to see. He recalled hearing that the color could change, but if there was ever any chance of passing the chit off as his, she'd do better with her mother's— and his own—blond hair. Now, if she did not develop a space between her teeth, Ty would be more relieved. "I thought newborns were supposed to be so ugly, all red and creased and pinched together. One of my men said his new son looked like a dried-up apple."

Delia smiled, but more at the treasure she held than at the viscount. She had never seen such a beautiful child, either. She had never seen as young an infant at all, single women generally being excluded from the birthing process, but she was certain this was the prettiest babe in all of England. "Perhaps they are injured when they are born in the usual fashion." Then she blushed, because this was not a topic she should be discussing with a man. His lordship was going to think she was the veriest strumpet. "Do you wish to hold her?" she asked.

What a question! She might have asked if he wished to have his other arm cut off. Ty busied himself donning the jacket that Winsted had retrieved, at a safe distance in case Miss Croft thought to hand the infant over. "Your nanny thinks she is going to die, doesn't she?" he asked.

"Nanny thinks we are all going to die. We are, of course, but I mean that Nanny always sees the dark side of things. Otherwise she would not have to keep praying, would she?"

"What do you think, about the baby?"

Delia shrugged. "I do not know. She is so small, and so still. Healthy babies make a lot more noise, Nanny says. They strengthen their lungs that way. They do not all start to suck immediately after birth, but soon. If the baby does not, if she is too weak or too young . . ." Her voice trailed off. They both knew what happened to a creature that would not nurse.

Reverend Anselm had turned to a different page in his prayer book. He called them into a circle close to the fire. "Ty, you have to name godparents for the baby, to watch out for your daughter's spiritual well-being."

Who better than the vicar himself, Ty's old friend? "Would you serve, Stephen? I cannot think of a better man for the job."

Mr. Anselm bowed. "I would be delighted."

"And Miss Croft, of course, if you would?"

"Since I cannot be her aunt, I would be pleased to be her godmother. Thank you, my lord, for the honor."

Anselm looked up from his prayer book. "And a name."

Ty's mind was blank. "A name?"

"We cannot christen her into the church without a name, old chap. The poor mite will want something on her birth certificate, you know." As usual, the vicar refused to consider that the name might soon be inscribed on a gravestone. "And as my first duty as godfather, I am begging you not to pick something like Clytemnestra or Calpurnia. She is too small for such a mouthful, for one, and I would not have her growing up defending herself against being called Clem or Cal."

Ty looked at the infant, but all he saw was Miss Croft, with that rapt, Madonna-like expression all women got when they held babies. She would make a good mother herself someday, he was certain, if she found a husband worthy of her.

"Would you wish me to call her Georgina?" he asked her. "Or Georgette, after her father?"

"What, and tell the whole world what we have been at pains to conceal?" Delia answered. "Definitely not."

"Shall I name her after her mother, then? Belinda?"

"The choice has to be yours, my lord. It is a pretty name."

And Belinda had been a pretty widgeon who could not count and had dreadful handwriting. Ty preferred not to immortalize her that way. "My mother's name was Melissa. How about Melinda? And Adele after her godmother? No one can object to that, can they?"

So Melinda Adele St. Ives was blessed and anointed from the bottle Anselm had so recently stoppered. And she complained. Nanny praised the Lord, but Mags rushed off to find Hessie Wigmore, who had given birth two months ago and had plenty of milk.

"But Hester was one of those who turned her back on Belinda," Delia fretted. "Will she come for Belinda's baby?"

"Mayhaps yes, mayhaps no. But she will come for Lord Tyverne's blunt. What with that ne'er-do-well Fred Wigmore for a husband and five children to feed, she'll come."

Just in case, Winsted was sent into the village to find out who had a milk cow for sale, and a nanny goat, too, for Mags declared some youngsters did better on one than the other.

While Delia, her aunt, and the nursemaid made lists of what the infant needed, and what might be found in the attics, Mr. Anselm was finally getting to pour himself that glass of brandy.

"I deserve it," he told his friend, who already had one in hand. "A marriage, a death, and a birth, all in one day. I've gone from giving last rites to performing a wedding, and once conducted a wedding and a christening in the same day. For the same couple, in fact. But I have never had to go through all three together. I doubt there could be anything else to top this."

The viscount was sipping from his own glass. "If the earl gets wind of it, you could add a suicide."

"No, knowing your father, it would be a homicide. Stivern will flay you alive for this day's work."

Ty took a larger swallow. "I did what I had to."

"Will you tell him?"

"What, travel to Warwickshire to inform my sire that he has a granddaughter, whom I could not possibly have sired? The blackguard is liable to use the marriage as proof that I am insane and incompetent, so he can push even harder to cut me out of the succession. No, the earl can read the announcement in the journals, the same as everyone else."

"Well, at least it is a girl."

Ty nodded. A common-born wife was bad enough. A bastard was worse. A bastard son bearing the St. Ives name would have been the worst complication of all. He raised his glass. "To a daughter. Now I can get on my way."

Chapter 17

"*W*hat do you mean, now you can be on your way?" Delia had come to urge the gentlemen to partake of the wedding breakfast in the dining room, whatever of it had not spoiled by now. The baby was asleep in her basket, once the dog had been ousted and fresh blankets laid there, and Delia realized she was hungry, herself. It had been a long, adventuresome, emotional morning. The men, especially a large man like Viscount Tyverne, must be sharp set. Instead, it seemed, he was set on leaving.

"I told you I had urgent affairs in London," he reminded her. "It is well past the time I wished to return. If I leave when Winsted gets back with the cow or goat or whatever, I can still complete most of the journey by nightfall."

"Your debt is paid, like a hotel bill, and now you will ride away, your obligations fulfilled?" Mags had said Viscount Tyverne was not the staying kind, but this was absurd. How could he go from tender comforter to callous cretin in a matter of minutes? The fact that he was a man, she supposed, was answer enough. Well, it was not good enough for her. Delia crossed her arms, set her jaw, and tapped her foot. "You are going to leave, just like that?"

Anselm bowed himself out of the room, the coward. Ty recognized the martial gleam in Miss Croft's green eyes, too, and thought enviously of the meal he knew was waiting below. Better a cold meal than this cold glare. He wondered what more the woman could want of him. What, did she expect him to change the infant's nappies next? He had done everything he could, dash it, and so he would tell her.

"Just like that, Miss Croft? I was intending to leave my man behind, with a blank check. I told him to reserve himself a room at the inn in the village, so not to be a burden to you here, but to be on hand to lend assistance."

"But what about the baby?"

Ty looked down at his flat chest. "Surely you are not suggesting I am equipped to care for the infant."

Delia looked down at her own regrettably meagerly endowed bust. "Surely you are not suggesting I am any better suited to the task."

Ty colored. Once again, he had stepped over the line, blast his barracks boorishness. "Forgive me, I was not referring to . . . to what the wet nurse provides. But surely she will have the care of the child."

"Hessie Wigmore is the poor wife of a poor hog farmer, who drinks besides. They live in a dirt-floored cottage, with some of his hogs, I have no doubt. Certainly Fred smells like one. Their children are dirty, rowdy, and runny-nosed. I cannot think you would wish to have Melly staying there."

"I thought we agreed the infant was to be named Melinda. And there is no question of her residing with the . . . the Wigmores and their livestock."

"No? Mrs. Wigmore is to live here, then, bringing her own brood along? Or simply come and go in the middle of the night when Melly is hungry? For that matter, if Melly does accept animal milk and a leather nipple, did you think Belinda's child would be welcome at Faircroft House when Clarence and Gwen and their own piglets, ah, children move in?"

"I, ah, thought that you—"

"You thought that I would keep your daughter with me."

"You seem fond of the br—baby. Melinda."

"Of course I am fond of Melly. That does not mean I can be a parent to her. If she fails to thrive, I would have no idea what to do." And if the tiny darling followed her mother, Delia had no idea how she could bear yet another loss of someone precious to her. She could not let herself love this little scrap of life.

"Lud, do you think I would know what to do for a sickly infant?"

"No, but you could hire experts. Here there is no one but Mags. I doubt if I will stay on at Faircroft anyway. You've met Cousin Clarence and his wife."

Ty nodded. He would not stay in the same village with those mushrooms, much less the same house.

"Aunt Rosalie will not take me in if I have a child in tow. She wants someone to fetch and carry, not clutter her drawing room with rattles and bibs."

Ty frowned, recalling the letter she'd written to George. "I assumed your aunt in London was to introduce you around, see to your presentation."

"I am well past the age for a come-out. And Aunt Rosalie might have done so at one time, but the opportunity never arose." It might have arisen, Delia could not help thinking, if her aunt was not too lazy to be a chaperone, too vain to consider herself a matron, and too clutch-fisted to throw a ball in Delia's honor. Delia was still angry with her aunt for those nip-cheese five pounds. "Now I am in mourning, of course."

As was he, Ty recalled. Lud, was he really wed and widowed on the same day? A soldier never had time to indulge in formal mourning—Zeus, he'd be forever tying black ribbons—but Ty supposed he ought to wear an armband for Belinda. He'd see to it as soon as he reached London. At this rate, he might never get there.

Miss Croft was going on: "Not that it is any of your affair, my lord, but I might not accept my aunt's offer, anyway. I have been thinking I might go into service, become a paid companion, instead of my aunt's unremunerated lackey. I doubt having an infant at hand is a boon to finding employment."

Miss Croft could not become a servant. Ty would not have it. This bright young woman, ground to a gray shadow by a life of servitude? Never. "I would pay—"

"What, you would pay my way?" That made Delia even madder, that this clench-mouthed clunch thought he could buy his way out of his obligations. "I can imagine how respectable I would appear then. A single young woman with a baby? No community in England would welcome us, nor believe Melly was not my child. Or did you assume I would take on the guise of a war widow? Either way, I would have scant opportunity to find a husband of my own, to have my own children instead of yours and Belinda's, or to live without being beholden to you. No, my lord, Melly is your daughter, and yours to look after. Besides, you saved her life. That in itself makes her your responsibility, much as I might wish it otherwise."

Ty worked on getting his jaw muscles to relax, so he could open his mouth. "I, ah, I had not thought." He'd thought Miss Croft looked so content with the babe in her arms that she would wish to keep Melinda, not that the infant might be a blight upon her life. He could see now that he had been wrong. An unmarried woman's condition was not an easy one, it seemed, with few options open to her, but many restrictions. No wonder so many were such avid husband hunters. "The easiest thing would be for us to marry."

Ty gasped. Had he really spoken that aloud? Now he wished his mouth had stayed permanently locked tight. So what if he ground his teeth to nubs?

Delia gasped, too. Of course it would be easy for this oaf to have a ready-made nursemaid, easy for him. "Of all the insulting offers—" she started.

"It . . . it was not actually an offer, Miss Croft," Ty hurried to say. "I was just thinking aloud, that you need a home and Melinda needs a mother and I need to be in London."

Not "I need you by my side for eternity." Not even "I need a wife." The man needed his ears boxed. Delia would have done it, too, except she was a lady, no matter what the red-jacketed jobberknowl thought.

The man kept addling her wits, he did, with his mercurial moods. Sometimes he showed her his gentlemanly side, so exemplary she almost wished he could love her. If Tyverne liked her even a little, she might be willing to risk a marriage of convenience, for Delia could see where she could come to love such a paragon. She knew the advantages of such a union, just as she knew how hard it would be to find a better match or a better man. She feared she'd measure every other male she met against Lord Tyverne's admirable standards—until he acted like an ape. He needed a nursemaid, did he? And an heir eventually. How lucky to find one woman for both positions! It was almost as fortunate as finding a horse that could both take a saddle and pull a coach. "I told you, my lord, I will not marry for material gain."

"I am not speaking merely of money, if I were indeed speaking of marriage, that is. You could keep the baby. You said you were fond of her."

"I am fond of Baron Dallsworth's formal gardens, but I will not marry him to get them, either."

"I suppose that is just as well. I doubt even I could get the archbishop to issue a third special license in a matter of days." Of course, there was no need to hurry, really. They could wait the month to call the banns. Six months would be more respectful of Belinda's memory. A year would satisfy the tabbies. But it was all hypothetical anyway. Miss Croft did not want him.

"Whatever debt you believed you owed my brother is paid in full," she was saying. "You do not need to enter another marriage of convenience on my behalf."

Ty was not about to explain how convenient he thought such a match might be, how easy he'd find it to look at Miss Croft's sparkling eyes and pink-stained cheeks across the breakfast table. Then his stomach growled at the mention of breakfast.

Delia must not have heard it, because she went on: "Your obligation is to your daughter now."

If he did not starve to death first, Ty thought. The woman must live on moonbeams, she was so slender. He nodded, though, and said, "I can see where I shall have to make other arrangements. But you must also see where I cannot simply pack Melinda and her basket into a carriage and drive to Town. I'll have to look into finding a comfortable family to take her in, which will be far easier to do in London. I can ask my sister to help, for one thing. She knows everyone. Although she has never had a child herself, Ann is bound to know how to locate a competent wet nurse, at least."

"And a nursery maid."

Ty looked toward the basket, too small to carry a substantial meal, but big enough to give him the headache. "And whatever else the child needs. But you do see that I cannot take her with me now, don't you? I shall speak to Sir Clarence again. Surely he can wait a week or two to move in, if I offer to have the place painted and papered for him. Lady Clarence will likely want the Egyptian style that's all the crack in London, I understand. I can promise to order a crocodile sofa for her while I am there."

Delia grimaced at the thought of her childhood home turned into a museum exhibit, but knew Gwen and Clarence would be thrilled. The only way they would be happier would be if Tyverne took them to London with him, instead of the baby. She nodded. "Melly can stay with the Wigmores at night for a week, I suppose, unless she takes to a bottle."

Ty was too relieved at her acquiescence to correct the child's name. "And Winsted will stay behind to help."

"Very well. But what about Belinda?"

"Hell, you do not expect me to take her to London, too, do you?"

Delia started tapping her foot again. "The funeral."

"What about the funeral?" They would be planning Ty's, if he did not eat soon. "Anselm said he would talk to the local chap, make sure the thing got done up right and tight. She will have a spot in the churchyard, and I will have them put the biggest headstone they can find there, if you want, so no one can say she died in shame."

"What about a coffin?"

"I told Winsted to make arrangements." There, Ty thought, she could not accuse him of neglecting his responsibilities.

"What, your sergeant? How will he know what kind of coffin you want, or what color lining?"

Dash it, a plain pine box was good enough for Ty and his friends. Obviously not for Miss Croft. "I will instruct Winsted."

"And flowers."

Ty looked around. The ones from the wedding looked fine to him. Almost good enough to eat. "Winsted can purchase more."

"Will you order your man to attend the service, too? No one else will come, you know."

"You—"

"Women are not encouraged to attend the grave site. We are supposed to sit home and prepare the burial repast."

Ty's stomach recognized that word, too. "Surely the neighbors will go," he said to cover the noise.

Delia shook her head. "Not once her father disowned her. Squire is a powerful man in the area, and everyone fears him. Belinda would be lowered into the ground with no one there to mourn her or to place a flower on the grave."

She sniffed once. It was enough.

"I suppose I can wait another day to leave for Town," Ty conceded. Damn and blast, he cursed to himself meanwhile, if a wife was this much trouble dead, he could only imagine what chaos a live one caused. The deuced funeral would be held tomorrow, if he had to buy a new roof for the blasted church. "I shall go into the village immediately to make the arrangements." And to have a meal at the inn.

"Good. And I can give you a list of what to purchase for Melly there, until we can get to the attics to see what is usable. Perhaps your man can help me this afternoon when you are in the village. Mindle is too old, you see, and your arm—"

The infant made a noise then, and Delia disappeared in the direction of the basket. The sound had not been half as loud as the rumblings from Ty's stomach, he groused, but she'd had no trouble hearing *that*.

Chapter 18

C ows and coffins and cribs. Ty knew as much of one as he knew of the other, and more about all of them than he wanted, by the end of the day.

He set off for the village on foot, since someone had turned Diablo out into a paddock, likely to save what was left of the stable stall walls. Winsted was already in the attics, and Ty was not up to catching the gelding, especially not after Diablo had been penned up for a few days.

The boy, Dover, accompanied him, as if his lordship might get lost between Faircroft and the nearby village, which was all of ten minutes down the high street. Perhaps Miss Croft feared he'd take a wrong turn, and just happen to end up in London. The boy was a good excuse, at any rate, for stopping at the bakery, which was not on Ty's list at all. The boy was scrawny and needed fattening up.

Dover did not need his vocabulary expanded, although that was what he got, when Ty discovered that the coffin—with pink silk lining—would not be ready for two days. Neither would the cemetery plot, since the diggers did not work on Sunday. If the viscount's arm were stronger, he'd have half a mind to dig the blasted hole himself. It would not be the first time he had buried a fallen comrade by the wayside. Of course Kent was not the wayside, and Belinda was his wife. Perhaps he could remember that salient fact if he repeated it often enough.

He did not feel married. Or widowed. He felt hungry. That was it, that was what was niggling at him, despite the two strawberry tarts, not a pair of green eyes.

Ty considered, on his way to the inn, having Miss Gannon—Lady Tyverne, dash it—cremated. That way her ashes could be sprinkled on George's grave, where they belonged, with no one the wiser.

No one but Miss Croft, he amended, who wanted a respectable interment for her disrespected friend. So be it. Ty never again wanted to see that look on Miss Croft's face, the one where surprise and disappointment mixed, as if her own pet had relieved itself on her foot.

Oh, yes, the dog was with them also. The walking white hair ball needed the exercise, Miss Croft had said. It was jealous of the baby, she said. It missed Belinda. Ty made sure the bow was off the creature's neck before he stepped out of the Faircroft House door. At least the dog's presence explained a stop at the butcher's for a meat pastry. The animal looked scrawny, too.

A lot of Ty's errands were easily accomplished at the inn. Tradesmen and townsfolk wanted to get a glimpse of Belinda Gannon's hero, so they ringed his table and shared his meal, and agreed to deliver whatever he needed to Miss Croft's residence. Of course, now that they were on speaking terms with a real lord, it would only be respectful to attend his wife's funeral. The fellow was not high in the instep at all, they decided, breaking bread and drinking ale with whomever approached him.

In no time at all, the viscount had black ribbons for mourning, pink ribbons for Melinda's cradle, and a new account at the local bank. He ordered a tombstone, to be inscribed with Belinda's name—and title, he made sure—and the word "Beloved" underneath. He tasted the milk from two cows without noticing a difference, so chose to buy from the needier-looking farmer. He refused to sample the goat's milk, but made Dover do it, then pretended not to notice when the boy gave the cup to the dog. The chosen animals were led off to Faircroft while Ty finished his lamb stew.

Leather nipples, small glass bottles, knit caps, cotton wool, yards of soft linen, and a doll, which was not on his list, either, but seemed something a girl child ought to have, all were to be at Miss Croft's by nightfall. Peppermint drops and rum balls—a lot of rum balls if he hoped to catch the horse—were in a sack Dover carried, along with a whistle and a top, which seemed some things a boy ought to have.

The list for Melinda went on and on, it appeared to Ty, a great deal of baggage for such a small being, and one who might not survive the first night. Dover was full of tales of orphaned infants at the foundling home who never made their first birthdays. Ty made the lad drink the rest of the cow milk, to stop the gloomy stories.

Flowers were not available, not unless Lord Tyverne wanted to apply to Baron Dallsworth and his glasshouses. The viscount did not. He sent one of the Whitaker boys from the inn into Dover—the city—with a wagon, to see what was for sale there. Another son was sent to London with a packet of letters Ty had written before leaving Miss Croft's. One was to his sister, but the other, much harder to compose, was to his man of affairs in Town. This one was the notice to be sent to the appropriate newspapers. Ty had deliberated long and hard whether to submit a betrothal, a birth announcement, or a bereavement notice. In the end, he chose the obituary, a very brief one, stating the death of Belinda Gannon St. Ives, Viscountess Tyverne, who was survived by her husband and infant daughter. That ought to set the cat among the pigeons nicely, Ty thought, as he handed a purse to the Whitaker lad.

Molly Whitaker would have given him her sons, not just lent them out for the afternoon, she was so taken with the handsome officer. Why, he'd taken the top rooms of her inn for his friends for the week, and paid a month's lodging for his man, in advance. And the Widow Whitaker did like to see a fellow who enjoyed her cooking.

Lord Tyverne enjoyed it so much, he ordered more

sent out to Miss Delia's, so her kitchens would not be overburdened with the extra mouths to feed. Stephen Anselm and the solicitor were staying for the funeral—Ty was paying the one and begging the other—and would expect a meal after the service, as would his new friends in town. Belinda would have a memorial befitting a viscountess, by Zeus, and by Ty's purse.

Black-bordered cards and handkerchiefs trimmed in black lace completed his shopping, and a huge slice of Widow Whitaker's gooseberry pie completed his meal. The viscount was ready to return, to bask in Miss Croft's approval for all he had accomplished, and to take a nap. Lud, this had been an endless day, after a sleepless night.

Unfortunately, however, at least one other local inhabitant had gotten wind of the viscount's visit to town. A thick-set, jowly fellow of middle years and pale eyebrows approached his table. "My name is Durwood Gannon, my lord, and we've got something in common."

Not by half, they did not. The man was wearing a loose brown fustian coat with yellowed linen beneath, scuffed boots with spurs, and an old-fashioned nut-brown bag wig. He carried a riding crop and a mug of ale. "Dover, take the dog outside," Ty ordered. "The mutt needs to walk after all you have slipped it under the table." To say nothing of what Ty had fed it.

The viscount nodded for the squire to sit down, without getting up or offering his hand, a sign of disrespect Gannon could not overlook.

"What is it you think we have in common, Squire?" he asked after signaling to Molly for another cup of coffee.

"Why, m'gel, of course. Everyone's talking about how you wed the chit afore she breathed her last. That's right, ain't it?"

"Only half. I did wed Miss Gannon, but she was not your anything. My understanding was that you had disowned the poor girl, precisely when she needed your support."

Gannon's face grew red, and he pounded his mug on the table, spattering a few drops of ale and making the riding crop bounce on the wooden surface. "The gel disobeyed me. And shamed me. What was I supposed to do?"

Ty kept his voice soft in contrast—in contrast to the rough countryman's bluster, and in contrast to the harsh, violent urges he felt toward this cur. He said, "You were supposed to do what any loving parent would have done, cared for her." Many would not, he knew, his own father included. Had his sister Ann chosen an unacceptable *parti*, Ty had no doubt, the earl would have had the fellow press-ganged, and Ann locked in her room until she wed the man of the earl's choice. If she'd found herself increasing, Lady Ann would have found herself on a ship for the Colonies before she could bring scandal and disgrace to the family name. No one said Stivern was a loving parent, though.

Ty wondered what he would do, when Melinda was of marriageable age. What if she wanted to marry someone beneath a viscount's daughter, someone like Dover, for instance? The boy was likable, intelligent, and bid fair to being handsome, once his teeth came in. His birth was no more irregular than Melinda's, except he did not know his parents. What would Ty do if she swore her world depended on a foundling? Well, he would not disinherit her, that was for sure. Not after struggling so hard to see her birth legitimized. The first thing he would do, the viscount decided, was get Dover a gentleman's education, starting next week.

Ty sighed. That was when he got to London. Gannon was here now. The man was neither loving nor wise. "It seems to me that if you had let Belinda marry her childhood sweetheart, none of this would have happened. They would not have anticipated their vows, and George would not have gone off to war." And Tyverne would be dead on a dusty field, but he could not think about that now. "You could have been dandling your grandchild on your knee, and Belinda would be living at Faircroft House, instead of waiting there for the undertakers' wagon to come."

"Well, that's all spilt milk, don't you know."

No, it was spilled ale making the table sticky. The dog had not left a drop of milk. Ty was sure Dover had taken the canine outside in time, besides. He sipped at his coffee, not replying.

"Yes, well, I, ah, thought we could come to terms now, you and me."

Ty got up to leave before his coat sleeve and his digestion were both ruined. "I would not come to you for a drink were I dying of thirst, sirrah, much less come to any kind of terms."

"But, but, I say, there's the matter of the settlements. We haven't touched on the matter yet."

"Settlements?" Ty asked in disbelief at the man's gall. "The contracts to establish her allowance and annuity, to provide for a wife if her husband predeceases her? Your daughter requires none such now."

Gannon flushed a deeper shade. "Aye, all that, but oftimes a gent offers his papa-in-law a settlement, too. He helps pay some of the bills for all the folderols and furbelows a female needs. Else he lets the chit's father manage the trust fund in exchange for the gel and her dowry."

"Oh, were you handing me Belinda's portion, then? I had not thought you so generous. But I thank you, no. I have no need for your money."

From the disconcerted expression on Gannon's face, he'd had no intention of paying out the *dot*. "The gel's dead."

"Precisely. So we have nothing to discuss. On the other hand, if you wish to set the sum aside for Belinda's daughter, my man will draw up the papers. Now that I think of it, most jointures are established to pass to a woman's descendants, not back to her father when she dies. My solicitor will call on you tomorrow, then. I am sure you will cooperate with him."

"Oh, old Heddy Hedgewick drew up the papers. No need to trouble him."

"Especially since, ah, Heddy is not my solicitor. Mr.

Macurdle is. A very thorough chap. I am certain you will find him knowledgeable in these matters. He will do everything in his power to see that the infant is well protected. Against every kind of viper."

Gannon's complexion suddenly lost all color, until Ty could finally see a resemblance between him and Belinda. "That's another thing," Squire said, not ready to give up despite Ty's steps away from the table. "M'granddaughter."

If Melinda was this dirty dish's granddaughter, then Ty was his son-in-law. Bloody hell. "No. Keep the dowry. If your daughter was stricken from your family tree, you cannot claim the sprout."

Gannon smiled, showing tobacco-stained teeth. "Never made it official, don't you know. I meant to rewrite m'will, but never got around to it, what with hunting season and the fall harvest. I used a pencil on the Bible, anyways. Erased it already, when I heard of the wedding."

"A ring on her finger made you love your daughter again? I will have to remember that, when Melinda comes of age."

Gannon could not figure Ty's meaning. "But . . . but what do you want with an infant? Especially one what's not your—"

He stopped when Ty held up his hand and quietly said, "Melinda is my daughter, is that plain?"

"Aye, and I wouldn't be here else. But a toff like yourself can't want a baby around, whether you go back to the army or go on the strut in London."

"And you do want the babe?"

"Aye, miss my girl, I do. She was my only company since m'wife passed on. I have plenty of room. Servants. A whole nursery done up in pink. I can locate Bel's old nursemaid, too."

"While I, of course, would underwrite the child's upbringing, finance her education and pay for those servants, governesses, music instructors, and French lessons. To say nothing of letting you have the interest from Belinda's bride portion. Or were you hoping I'd go back to the Peninsula and get myself killed, leaving her an heiress?"

Gannon was on his feet now, too. "You are going to farm her off to strangers anyways. At least with me she'd be with blood kin."

What good had relatives been to Belinda, Ty wondered, or Delia, for that matter? Or him? This dastard had raised a flighty female. Worse, he'd cruelly disowned her. Worst of all, he was fool enough to think Ty would hand him another innocent to destroy. He'd see him in hell before—

"I will see you at Belinda's funeral in two days. She would have liked that, I think." Delia would, and the villagers would cease some of their gossip if they saw Belinda's father there, as if he had given his blessings on the marriage.

"And the babe?" Gannon pressed.

"Is well. Thank you for asking."

Chapter 19

*D*elia wished she could have gone into the village with Lord Tyverne, but the old tabbies' soup bowls were already overflowing with scandalbroth. No need to add any more spice to the brew. She watched from the upstairs window as the viscount strode away down the path, then adjusted his long steps to let Dover keep up with him. The boy had begged her for permission to accompany his new hero, and even Belinda's dog had whined to follow.

Up in the attics, she had to listen to Sergeant Winsted sing his major's praises. The older man admitted he was not quite accustomed to civilian life, but swore he would follow his officer anywhere.

"Like as not, though, the major will sell out, on account of his bad arm and the fevers."

"Surely there are positions for an officer that do not involve wielding a sword and a pistol at the same time."

"Aye, but Major Tyverne ain't one to sit at a desk, nor stay behind the lines. He's never sent men into battle yet, not without himself at the head of the column."

Then Delia was subjected to Aunt Eliza's paean to the peer's perfection. Lord Tyverne had taken her aunt's order of new handkerchiefs with him, it seemed, as if he were a footman doing errands. "And he would not hear of taking my pin money to pay for them, either, the dear man, saying he owed me more, for my care of Belinda."

Just thinking of the viscount's kindness was enough to bring tears to Aunt Eliza's eyes.

Even Nanny and Mags had changed their tunes. The old nursery maid declared Lord Tyverne a decent, God-fearing gentleman. His language could use a scrub brush, but his soul seemed pure. Wasn't he moving heaven and earth to see that unfortunate girl buried in sanctified ground? Mags now believed he was as steady as sunrise, his word as good as the gold band he had placed on Miss Gannon's finger—and the gold in Mags's hand, for her services. "You can trust a real gentleman like that, Miss Dilly, to do what's right."

Delia was not jealous, of course, that Tyverne seemed to attract adulation like a fine actor drew applause. She had to admit he really was an honorable man, always. And kind, usually. Easy to deal with? Sometimes. Bendable? Hah! But she was not jealous that even Mindle was considering asking the viscount for a position, after Sir Clarence and his wife moved into Faircroft House.

Nor was she envious of Hester Wigmore's large breasts. Well, perhaps . . . No, Delia told herself, she would fall over on her face with such forward ballast.

She did not resent the sow-scented Hessie's ability to sooth baby Melinda and send her back to sleep, either.

No, what turned Miss Croft nearly green with jealousy was the fact that Tyverne and Dover got to go to the village, the women all got to stay upstairs admiring Melly, and Mindle got to inspect the wine cellar for the viscount's dinner—while she had to entertain Cousin Clarence.

Clarence and Gwen had arrived, they said, to reassure Delia that another week or so before their occupancy would not be a terrible inconvenience. Not after receiving the viscount's message, it would not. From their satisfied smirks, Delia gathered the man could have purchased an abbey for what he was paying these two in rent.

They also came to bring a gift to the baby, a coral

teething ring, the same one, Delia believed, she had
given their youngest offspring three or four years previously. So she asked if she should send for little Melinda
St. Ives, so Gwen might hold her.

Gwen was already holding the Sèvres vase, trying to
read the mark on the bottom without tipping out the
water and flowers. "What, in this gown?" Gwen was
wearing a sky-blue silk dress today, with a jonquil lace
overskirt. She did have on black lace gloves and a fringed
black lace shawl for mourning. Clarence matched, in a
blue coat, yellow Cossack pants, with a black silk ro-
sette boutonniere.

Delia had changed into her unrelieved black.

She was not surprised Gwen did not wish to hold the
infant. After all, Clarence's wife had rarely held her own.
Nursemaids, governesses, and tutors had the rearing of
the Croft offspring while Gwen had naps, dress fittings,
and crushed strawberry face masques. Delia hoped Lord
Tyverne would do better for Melly. Her goddaughter deserved a loving home, with people who truly cared for
her. It would be too easy for the viscount to install Melinda at one of his family estates with nothing but servants for company, the way he was raised. She might
grow up like him then, knowing plenty about propriety,
and aught of affection. Poor little girl.

And poor Delia, as Gwen swooped around the drawing room, making mental notes for redecorating. That is,
Gwen did the thinking, when she was not untangling her
shawl from the chair-back finials or the window-hanging
tie rods. Delia was supposed to be recording the instructions, so she could be hiring workers, sending for fabric
samples, ordering the wall hangings . . . and living in
total disarray.

"I am afraid all that will not be possible, Cousin,"
Delia told her. "Plaster dust and new paint are so un-
healthy for infants, don't you know. His lordship could
not mean to have Melinda in jeopardy while he makes
arrangements for her future."

"Surely the nursery is far enough away." Gwen obviously had no intentions of refurbishing the nursery for her own progeny.

"Oh, but Melinda's cradle will never be so distant. And I shall be spending most of my time looking after her, of course. Besides, I am certain you will want to oversee the renovations for yourself, to make sure everything is up to your high standards." Faircroft House would look like a sultan's tent, by Gwen's standards, but Delia hoped to be gone by then. Fetching Aunt Rosalie's smelling salts and embroidery yarns had to be better than watching Gwen destroy her family home. Of course, there was still Nanny's future to worry about, and Aunt Lizzie's.

Then another option arose.

"Lord Dallsworth," Mindle announced.

Delia glared at Clarence, but he hunched his fleshy shoulders, which did little for the fit of his coat. "I wasn't the one to invite him to visit, not after Tyverne took him in aversion. Though I cannot see what it matters to the viscount now. Married Belinda, didn't he, not you? Could have been Lady Tyverne yourself, by Jupiter, if you'd done something about your dress and your hair. And your tongue." Clarence's tongue was wrapped around a peeled orange, or a pomander, depending on one's point of view.

By her preening and posturing, Clarence's wife must have been the Croft who encouraged Delia's unwanted caller. Gwen held out her hand for kissing, or drooling on, as Dallsworth was wont to do, and ordered Mindle to fetch tea.

If Gwen liked Dallsworth so well, Delia wondered, why did she not simply run off with the man?

He was too old to run, for one thing; the notion of prunes-and-prisms Gwen setting herself up as a topic of gossip was so ludicrous, for another, that Delia had to hide a chuckle behind her hand, which she reclaimed from Dallsworth before he could bring it anywhere near his thin, wet lips.

He asked for her hand again, anyway. In marriage, that is.

The baron was tall but stooped, with failing eyesight, so he always appeared to be peering up through straggly brows, or leering down a lady's décolletage. He had more hair in his eyebrows than he had on his head, but each strand there was carefully pomaded in place for maximum coverage. His clothes were old-fashioned and ill-fitting, and he must bathe as often as Hessie's hogs, to judge from his odor. His ardor, also, offended.

Dallsworth's wife had died three years previously, leaving him with no heir, no readily available, free bed partner, and no competent housekeeper. He did not want to bother going up to London to find some silly young miss who would not know how to run a household, or who would be pining to run off to parties and such. He definitely did not want some pretty widgeon who'd have her head turned by the first handsome buck to pass through the neighborhood.

Miss Delia Croft suited him to a cow's thumb. She was sensible, efficient, and no beauty to catch a man's fancy. In fact, the baron admired Delia's dowry more than her red-haired looks. He preferred his females to be better cushioned, but there were always Dover dockside doxies when a man wanted a cozy armful, not a bony begetting. Delia would be a respectable mother to his heir, now that the disgraceful matter of her brother's whore was concluded. He was impressed that she'd gotten Tyverne to wed the wench, boding well for Miss Croft's potential as a political hostess. Yes, she'd serve satisfactorily as Baroness Dallsworth, and she would serve the baron, too. He licked his lips, and not over the tea tray the butler was carrying in.

He wanted the Croft chit and her dowry, and he wanted them now, before either of them got any older. "Now that you have held an infant in your arms, my dear," he told her when she brought his cup of tea, "I am certain you will be eager to have one of your own."

Delia was eager to go hold Melinda again, anyway.

"As am I," Dallsworth went on. "We could share the reward of bringing forth a new life."

A child, in this man's image? They would both drool, for sure.

"I could not press my suit during the regrettable interval just passed, not with my political position to uphold, you understand, but once the viscount removes the, ah, child, there will be nothing to come between our marriage of true minds, heh-heh."

Delia could think of a hundred things, half of them likely living in his unwashed linen. "I am sorry, my lord, but—"

Seeing all hope for a government appointment falling by the wayside, Clarence put down his poppy seed cake long enough to say, "You had ought to consider his lordship's offer more seriously this time, Dilly. Might be your last chance at the pleasures of motherhood, don't you know, and having a place of your own."

And getting out from under Gwen's thumb, too, Delia had to acknowledge.

The baron sweetened the offer, with a sour-breathed smile. "I might be willing to foster the infant for St. Ives when he returns to the army."

Delia did not say that she'd rather see Lord Tyverne take Melinda back to the Peninsula than let Dallsworth touch the beautiful child. "I understand he is thinking of resigning his commission," she said instead.

"No matter. He will be a widower on the Town then, heh-heh, target for every marriage-minded miss and her mother. And what lady—for Stivern will demand nothing less for his heir the second time—would want to raise another woman's child?" He sipped his tea; Belinda's dog lapped less audibly. "Much less one who is a . . . heh-heh."

"A bastard?" Delia asked, setting her own cup down. "I daresay Miss St. Ives will never be addressed as such. When the Earl of Stivern passes on, in fact, I believe Melly will become Lady Melinda. If she has half of her mother's beauty and her father's charm, she will be acclaimed a Belle. When her father dowers her as generously as I assume he will, she will be called a Toast, able to look as high as she pleases for a husband of her own. Why, her aunt is a duchess. Do you truly think anyone will cast aspersions on her birth?"

The baron thought Delia Croft looked almost desirable when she had some fire in her blood instead of the ice water she usually displayed. He licked his lips again. "No, of course not. She'll make a fine playmate for our own gels, hm?"

"So you'll need to take Nanny with you," Clarence put in, happy to be saved from sending his old nursemaid to the poor house, or—he almost choked on a bite of lemon tart at the thought—pensioning her off.

"And your aunt Eliza," Gwen eagerly added, anxious to remove all of the outré females from her house. "I am certain the dear baron would welcome Miss Linbury with open arms."

Delia was certain Dallsworth would welcome Melinda, Nanny, and Aunt Eliza as much as he'd welcome another wart on his nose, but Aunt Rosalie in London was less than likely to invite any of Delia's *menage* at all.

"Handsome offer, I would say," Clarence did say. "You won't get a better one, now that you've whistled the viscount down the wind." He wolfed down a macaroon.

Undoubtedly, Delia acknowledged, she would not find a more expedient solution to her difficulties. Yet, if she would not marry an eminently honorable gentleman to secure her future, how could she wed someone whose very handshake, hygiene, and heh-hehs repulsed her? The thought of sharing Dallsworth's bed was—What was worse than repulsive? Nauseating? Worms crawling between your toes? Screeching bats tangled in your hair?

She shook her head to clear the horrid images, and recalled a large, fair-haired gentleman stretched out on a makeshift bed instead. Half dead from the fevers, Lord Tyverne had still made a more appealing picture than Dallsworth, dirty and drooling. The viscount was too appealing, in fact, and the notion of him in his bed, or in her bed, was too intriguing. Her imagination left the conversation far behind.

Gwen was planning the nuptials. "It will have to be a quiet wedding, I suppose," she said with regret, fingering the fringe of her black shawl.

Dallsworth nodded. "Just family and closest friends. And a few party cronies who might be of use to Sir Clarence, heh-heh. I can have the vicar start calling the banns tomorrow, what? And we can have the wedding in a month. What say you?"

"I say," came from Lord Tyverne in the doorway, "that Miss Croft will not be available."

Chapter 20

$\mathcal{T}$he last time Viscount Major Tyverne had stood in the Crofts' drawing room like a general inspecting his troops—and finding them sorely wanting—he had announced his betrothal to Delia. If he did that again, she swore to herself, make a high-handed declaration without her say-so, she might just accept the baron's proposal, just to prove to Lord Tyverne that he did not have the ordering of this recruit. Of course she would cry off before the cat could lick its ear—or Clarence could lick the crumbs off his chin—because there was no use destroying her life to make a point. Still, the cavalier cockscomb did not command Miss Croft. He could not purchase her cooperation, nor could he intimidate her. He—

Was inviting her to London.

First Squire Gannon, Ty was thinking, now Sir Clarence and Lord Dallsworth, all in one day. How did a man get so lucky? He already condemned Clarence for half his problems, and the empty dishes on the tea tray did not endear the baronet to him one whit. Dallsworth he despised on sight. The man was a dirty dish if the viscount ever saw one, filthy, fifty if he was a day, and fondling Miss Croft with his leer. The valiant female was holding her ground for now, chin in the air, eyes sparkling, but the hyenas would wear her down. Ty could not go to London, after the blasted funeral, leaving

George's sister with this pack of scavengers. Not if he wanted to sleep well at nights, he couldn't.

Sleep, night, and Miss Croft were a heady combination. The more Ty thought of it, the more he wanted the woman in London where she could be cared for and comfortable. Cherished, that's what she deserved to be, not hounded and harried by this scurvy lot. She also ought to be close to him. Very close, where a good night's sleep was the last consideration.

He bit his lip. A gentleman controlled his baser urges, and his mental images, or took a lot of cold baths. Unlike Dallsworth, obviously, Ty liked hot, soapy water, and he liked having a rational mind, a disciplined body. He was no lusting lad, and Miss Croft was a lady. There was something about the woman, however, that shook him from his senses to his stockings.

Ty was not about to rush his fences this time, though. "I have written to my sister," he told the assembled company, "and asked if I might bring the infant to her home once the child can travel, and until better arrangements can be made. I thought Miss Croft would come along to assist."

"What, Cousin Dilly travel with you to Town?" Gwen took out her fan and cooled her face, and the tea. "La, that is not at all the thing."

Ty had thought to send a carriage for them when he got back to London, as soon as his brother's argle-bargle was resolved. Now he decided he better ride alongside the coach. "With Nanny and Miss Eliza Linbury as chaperone, I believe your cousin's reputation will be preserved. The great debt I owe her brother would ensure my every care for her good name."

"And then," Clarence wanted to know, in case he was expected to send a coach for all of them to return, "once they get there?"

"Why, then my sister will need assistance with the child. She never had one, to her regret." The fact that neither had Miss Croft made no never mind. "I doubt her household is equipped, either." Ann was a duchess; she could order the moon and have it delivered on the instant, with enough servants to see to the unpacking. That was not the point. "And Miss Croft can help me select a more permanent home for the infant, interview families, that sort of thing. I expect it to take a month or more, to make the right choice."

"Yes, but then?" Clarence persisted, wondering if he could still negotiate a contract with Lord Dallsworth.

"After that if your cousin and my sister find they suit, perhaps Miss Croft will consider staying on. The duke travels a great deal, and my sister is alone too often."

Nanny, Aunt Eliza, and Delia out of the house all at once? Gwen thought the idea marvelous. Why, with their cousin connected to a duchess, who knew what invitations and opportunities would fall Sir Clarence's way? "Perhaps we might come to Town ourselves, to lend our expertise. Especially since Faircroft will be undergoing renovations. Dilly reminded us how insalubrious such things can be," Gwen hinted, then waited for an invitation. Her tea would grow a lot colder before one was forthcoming.

"No, no, I cannot like the idea," Lord Dallsworth said. "Miss Croft living at your sister's that way, with the infant, there is bound to be gossip. Miss Croft's reputation will suffer. It will not do, not at all."

Ty looked hard at the old goat. "I cannot see where it is your concern, and that is the truth." Then he finally turned to Delia, afraid he'd overstepped the bounds again, afraid she would say no, afraid she would say yes and foul up the rest of his life. "What say you to the notion, Miss Croft? Will it serve?"

At least someone thought to ask her opinion, Delia fumed, tired of the others discussing her future as if she were not there. But, yes, an invitation to his sister's just might do very well indeed. To the devil with Lord Tyverne's debts and obligations, this would not be charity. The duchess would not want the care of an infant on her hands, so would appreciate Delia and Nanny and Aunt

Eliza. After that, Delia would have to see. She had her doubts that the viscount's sister required a companion, but one of her friends might, or Her Grace might give Delia a reference. Meantime, Delia would dearly like to spend more time with little Melinda, to make certain the new family Tyverne chose for her was a loving one. Maybe they would grant Delia the occasional visit with the child, who was her goddaughter, after all. If she were honest with herself, she would not mind spending more time with his lordship, to see if he really did decide to sell out. And perhaps, just perhaps, by the way Lord Tyverne was gnawing on his lower lip, perhaps her answer really mattered to him.

"Yes, it might serve, my lord. I shall be pleased to consider your sister's invitation." Then she added, wondering if the managing major's sister even knew of the proposed visit, "When it arrives."

Ty had to be content with that. At least Miss Croft did not seem averse to London, although he could not tell if the baby were the carrot, or Dallsworth, et al., were the stick, or if he had anything whatsoever to do with her decision.

He also had to move to the inn in the village. The poor girl had suffered enough lectures from her relatives, for one thing. If he stayed, she would have to invite her encroaching relatives to dine, too, for another. No one deserved that.

So Ty saddled Diablo. Someone had put the big white gelding back in his stall, groomed and fed, but Jed Groom refused to get him tacked.

"Lost me a new shirt, last time I tried. Could of lost me an arm, iffen the devil was fresh."

The viscount's wounded arm was now strong enough to manage the sack of sweets, while his other hefted the saddle and tightened the girth. After a minor disagreement over who was in charge, and who paid for the delicacies, Ty rode to the village livery stable, where the ostler politely doffed his cap.

Ty rode back to Miss Croft's.

"I must apologize," he said when she left off her study of the new cow to see why he had returned to the stable.

Perhaps he was going to rescind the invitation, Delia thought, and wished to do so out of anyone else's hearing. Or maybe the dratted horse had tossed him. She studied the viscount carefully for injuries or grass stains, but he appeared more handsome than ever with his blond hair in disarray from the ride. Maybe he just wanted to spend more time in her company.

"And I must beg yet another favor. Will you keep Diablo here? They refuse to take him at the livery. Someone on your staff seems to have the knack of handling the brute, though, exercising him and such."

Delia scowled at the gelding, who was lapping at a dish of ale while Ty awkwardly took the saddle off again and brushed him down. From having a brother, she knew better than to offer assistance. "Of course. We'll manage."

"In fact, I would be willing to hire the fellow if he is interested and if you can spare him." He looked at Delia's old mare, the empty spaces for the carriage horses Sir Clarence and his wife had commandeered, and the cow and the goat that now shared the stable. Anyone who could deal with Diablo was wasted here. "I'll double his salary."

Delia bit back a word she had overheard George once use. "I will pass that on," she said instead.

"Are you quite sure the horse belongs to me?" Ty asked. "I would be happy to leave him here, permanently, if not. Your brother never truly gave me his mount. It was more in the manner of a loan, you know."

Delia grinned. "And I know you are wishing both of them to Hades. But, yes, I am certain George meant you to have the horse. The fact that you rode him to town and back is proof enough he is yours."

Ty walked back to the inn. The same road was growing tedious after five trips in one day. On the other hand, he thought he'd never be bored watching the fading light shimmer through the dark red curls that had escaped Delia's coiled topknot. He would definitely never weary of waiting for one of those glorious smiles that showed the intriguing space between her front teeth.

Ty walked back to Faircroft House the next day, in order to walk back to church with the ladies. The biggest gossip in the village could not find fault with that. Of course the biggest gossip in the village was Gwen, who rode in the Croft family carriage, despite living closer to St. Jerome's. He might be on his way to church, but his lordship's thoughts were anything but holy. For a cavalry officer, Major Tyverne was doing a deuced lot of marching: he had the sores to prove it. Worse, he went to the wrong pew. The Earls of Stivern commanded the first row of seats in at least three churches, two chapels, and a restored abbey, but this church was not one in their living. Here Dallsworth sat alone in the prestigious first pew, the only cushioned one. Squire Gannon sat, also alone, in the third pew. The Croft baronetcy merited the second, so Ty was sandwiched between two men he would cheerfully have consigned to the devil, on this the Sabbath. Worst of all for Ty's spiritual well-being, he was seated between Miss Croft and her aunt. No, his thoughts were not at all sacred. Blisters and blackguards and beguiling smiles, by Heaven. Or not.

Belinda's funeral the next day was all one could have wished for—unless, of course, one wished there was no need for a funeral. There were flowers and bell ringers and fancy handles on the coffin. The day was even overcast and drizzly, befitting the solemnity of the occasion, and no one doubted Lord Tyverne had ordered that, too. Stephen Anselm returned to share the duties with the local vicar, and most of the men of the village came out for the ceremony. Belinda's father wept copious tears: not only was he never going to see his daughter again, he was never going to see her dowry again, either.

Afterward, the men and their wives proceeded to Faircroft House. The funeral meal should by rights have been served at Squire Gannon's, not Miss Croft's, but Tyverne would not have accepted, had the man offered. Everyone in the village already knew of the connection anyway, so there was no more gossip than usual, and no less.

The house was so full of mourners, some had to drink Molly Whitaker's ale outside on the lawns. Gwen fluttered through the drawing room in layers of gauzy black netting, while Sir Clarence stationed himself in the dining parlor, where plates and platters and pitchers had been set out.

Wearing her best black gown, a black lace shawl, and her mother's locket, Delia was in looks. She was better rested than in weeks, it felt, and a certain anticipation added a glow to her smile. She accepted insincere compliments along with the insincere condolences, but held Tyverne's unspoken yet obvious admiration in her heart like a rare orchid.

She held the baby, too. Let the self-righteous old shrews of the neighborhood see what a beautiful, precious gift Belinda had bestowed on her husband, Lord Tyverne. She moved over to where he stood with Mr. Anselm, near the fireplace. "Here, my lord, would you like to hold your daughter?"

He'd rather jump in the grave with his wife. "No, my bad arm, you know."

"Nonsense, I have seen you riding Diablo, remember."

Anselm was grinning. Delia was holding out the pink-wrapped bundle. Ty was sweating. "Go on, old man," the viscount's former friend teased. "You've faced down the French. How much more courage does it take to hold an infant?"

More than Ty had. He shook his head. "No, I—"

"Take her," Delia hissed in a sharp whisper. "Hold her so they all see you are not ashamed of her."

He let the Croft fiend—ah, female—place the baby in his arms. "Just watch her head," she told him.

Horrified, Ty asked, "Why, is it going to fall off?"

But the baby's head stayed right where it was supposed to, and half the women dabbed at their eyes at the tender scene. The other half smirked when Melinda did what infants often did, on his lordship's scarlet regimentals.

Well, Ty thought, now he truly had to resign his commission.

Chapter 21

*H*e was on his way to London, at last. Ty had left behind his horse, his man, and his purse. Lud, he had not spent this much blunt in three years of soldiering. He felt as if he were financing the restoration of every building in Kent, from the church to the inn to Sir Clarence's house to Hessie Wigmore's cottage. He added checking on his investments to the long list of things he had to do in London.

Ty had also left his new daughter, of course and, he feared, part of his mind. He'd vowed to return in less than a week with a more comfortable carriage than this hired one, a baggage wagon, a cart to transport the cow and/or the goat, or a wet nurse if one were needed, the invitation from his sister, and more money. But he was forgetting something. The viscount did not know what it was, but some tiny detail, some lapse was niggling at the edge of his thoughts.

What he had gained from the short venture to Kent—Gads, was it less than a week?—besides a daughter, of course, was a black armband, Dover, and a dog.

"What do you mean, the animal is mine?" he'd demanded of Miss Croft when she handed him a satchel containing the creature's brush, bowl, and leather lead.

Delia was fluffing up the dog's white fur. "Why, she was your wife's pet. Of course she belongs to you, as all of Belinda's property and possessions would, if she had any. George bought the pup for Belinda before he left, so there is no question of Squire Gannon claiming her. Belinda named her Angelina to match Diablo, so it is only fitting you have both. Besides, you cannot think that Clarence means to keep her here, can you? His ill-mannered children would torment the poor little thing if he did."

"Then you keep her." Mindle had barely managed to make the viscount's uniform presentable. Ty did not need the blasted thing covered in white hairs now. "That's it, I shall deed her to you as a remembrance of your friend. A bequeathal, for your loyalty and care. Miss Gannon, Lady Tyverne, that is, would have wanted you to have the dog."

Delia shook her head and gave the terrier one last pat. "No, she seems to have adopted you as her new owner. Cook swears Angel has gone into a decline just since you moved to the inn, she is so off her feed."

The dog was not eating in the kitchens because Ty and Dover had fed her at the inn, the bakery, and the butcher's. After the funeral, she'd eaten more than Sir Clarence, by Jupiter. He took the satchel, but made Dover carry the dog.

The boy, it seemed, was another of his inheritances. Ty had intended to see to Dover's education, not become his guardian. It seemed Sir Clarence was not going to keep the foundling around, either, though, so as not to contaminate his own children with Dover's base origins.

"Furthermore," Miss Croft told him as she bent to straighten the boy's cap one last time, "we took him in to run errands for Belinda, so I suppose he is as much yours as the dog is."

So Ty had to hire the carriage, instead of riding Diablo hell-for-leather. That was the only speed the horse seemed to know, and would have suited the viscount perfectly, he was so late in getting to his brother. Instead, they had to stop every twenty minutes or so for the boy or the dog to piss.

At the second such stop, Ty got out to stretch his

legs, stiff from being confined in the narrow carriage, and realized that the troubling prickle was growing worse the further they got from Faircroft. For the life of him, Ty could not think what he could have forgotten. He was too good a soldier, though, to ignore the tingle between his shoulder blades, the intuition that something was wrong.

As he paced, he went over his leave-taking: Aunt Eliza's tears had not even given him a qualm, so enured was he; Nanny's prayers and godspeeds had drifted past, as had Winsted's assurances that he was on sentry duty until the major's return. Mindle had bowed with great dignity, smoothly accepting the coin Ty passed him. And Miss Croft . . . had not believed him.

That was it. Delia did not believe Ty was coming back. Oh, she assumed he would fetch the baby eventually, and his horse sooner, he thought, but she did not credit his vows of a speedy return and a welcome for her in London. Tyverne, whose word was his bond, could not accept that anyone could doubt his sworn oath, but there it was. He'd seen the doubt shadow her green eyes, dimming their radiance. He'd accepted the polite, distant wishes for his journey. He'd missed her smile; that's what he'd left behind.

Miss Delia Croft's brother must have ridden off in similar fashion, amid tears and prayers and promises to return. He had not.

Miss Croft did not, therefore, trust soldiers. Or maybe men. Between Sir Clarence, Dallsworth, and Squire Gannon, she had not found a chap whose word was worth tuppence. She simply had to be taught otherwise.

He ordered the driver to turn the carriage around.

Delia was in the stable, talking to Diablo. The conversation had cost her six carrots and a glove, but now, perhaps, the gelding did not feel as if he had been abandoned. If only a handful of vegetables could work for her.

The baby was sleeping, watched over by no less than

four doting females, and Delia was alone with her thoughts, which were not good company. She might always be alone, she worried, never get to hold Melly when a new family claimed her. Never hold an infant of her own. Never know a man. Never know love. She very much feared that her best chance for any of it had just driven away in a hired coach.

He was never coming back. He'd send for Melinda, see Delia and her dependents settled with his sister, but that was all. His sense of honor and obligation would be fulfilled. Then he'd go back to the army in one capacity or the other, or take up the gay life of London Society. In a month or two, a year at the most, Lord Tyverne would forget Miss Delia Croft existed. When would she forget the image of him smiling down at her, sharing his awe at the baby he held? Never.

Mindle said Miss Croft was in the stable. Zeus, Ty hoped she was nowhere near the unpredictable Diablo, whose mischief and meanness were all too foreseeable. He strode in that direction, also hoping that he could think of the right words to say before he got there. He was in mourning; she was in mourning. He was a wooden block around women; she thought all men were maggots. Those right words would be hard for Shakespeare to find. Still, Ty damned his clumsy tongue for going numb and his feeble wits for going begging, just when he needed them.

There she was, in the shadows of the stable outside Diablo's stall, wearing a dark green riding habit. This was the first time Ty had seen her out of mourning, and she looked magnificent to him. Her red hair was in a long braid down one shoulder, and she wore no hat and one glove. If he had found the words to tell her that he was going to come back, that she must not marry Dallsworth in the meantime or run off with Melinda to the Antipodes, the phrases melted away in the warmth of the welcoming, wondering smile she bestowed on him.

"I . . . I . . ." he started, taking up her bare hand. "I . . . Oh, hell." He pulled her hand, and her whole person, toward him and lowered his head until their lips touched. She did not back away or struggle, so he kissed her until neither of them had breath left, until they would both have fallen except for the stall door behind her, until she understood what he could never say.

"I *shall* return."

He was too late. For all of Ty's rushing, his bobbing block of a baby brother had gone and betrothed himself to a Bird of Paradise. The engagement of the Honorable Agamemnon St. Ives to Miss Thea Dunsley was announced in the same newspapers as Belinda, Lady Tyverne's, obituary.

"Dash it, Nonny," Ty said as soon as he'd seen the notice, which was within minutes of entering St. Ives House in Mayfair, thanks to an officious, starched-up butler who had been presiding over the house for decades, "you swore you would do nothing foolish until I got back."

"And so I have not." Nonny had one of those quizzing glasses the Town bucks favored and was scrutinizing Ty's bewhiskered coat.

It was bad enough that Nonny had gone back on his word, and worse, that he'd embroiled them all in yet another scandal. Worst of all, he was condemning himself to a lifetime of misery with a demimondaine for a wife. Furious, Ty pounded the newspaper on the desk between them. "If this misalliance is not foolish, I do not know what is! You promised to wait."

Nonny let the glass dangle on its ribbon. "I promised I would not run off to Gretna Green with Thea before you returned. I did not."

"Splitting hairs, brother. You knew I meant to convince you of the unsuitability of this match. You simply cannot marry a woman so far beneath you!"

Nonny tapped the newspaper. "You dare to lecture

me? It seems an instance of the pot calling the kettle black, *brother*."

"The situations are not at all the same."

"No, you are the heir while I am a mere third son. I can take Thea to live near Totty in the Americas, where no one has to know her past. You, on the other hand, cannot flee. You will be earl one day, fully in the sight of Society. Yet you, noble Ty, you have wed a rustic young female whose family no one has ever heard of, a female, moreover, who gave birth to another man's brat, upon which you bestowed our illustrious family name. Even if you are going to claim that Miss—what was her name?—was traveling with the army and carried your babe, do not speak of unsuitable females, Ty. A Hottentot could not be a less fitting viscountess. And do not speak of scandals. My engagement might cause a flurry, but your marriage is a veritable blizzard of *on-dits*. Mine might be the nails in the coffin, but your little escapade will surely send our father to an early grave. The earl will be so mad his blood will boil right in his veins. The only things that might save him from apoplexy is that the child is a girl, and your bride did not survive the honeymoon."

Ty straightened the newspaper in front of him. Poor Belinda had not even survived the wedding night. "My marriage was different. It was an affair of honor."

Nonny straightened his spine. "So is my engagement. Thea's name was being bandied about until I felt I must give her the protection of mine. The real difference is that I love her. You never even knew Miss whomever, did you?"

"It is Miss Gannon, and whether I knew her for a sennight or a century is irrelevant, dash it. We are not speaking of my marriage; we are speaking of yours, by Zeus. You are too young to be wed. You have no career, and no income other than what the earl or I provides. How are you going to keep your lady bird in fancy feathers?"

"Do not speak of Thea in that tone!"

Heedless, Ty went on: "When you are ready to take a wife, you will find one with a dowry, lands, a well-respected name."

"Like the duke's daughter Father wanted you to wed?" Nonny asked with a sneer. "Or the cabinet minister's girl? You did not jump at either chance. What did Miss Gannon bring to your match, then, my lord Tyverne, besides a bastard?"

"Dash it, do not speak of Belinda in that tone," Ty echoed, "or of my daughter. What Belinda brought me cannot be measured in pounds and pence, and I have need of neither." He did not want to mention the dog, or Dover, or the treasure that was Miss Croft's kiss. "Once and for all, we are not speaking of my marriage but yours. A gentleman simply does not marry his mistress!"

Nonny pounded on the desk. "You do not know what you are talking about. Just like Father, you've made your mind up without letting me explain."

Ty pounded the desk, too, enraged to be compared to the earl. "What is there to explain, dash it? You met the woman in Sukey Johnson's brothel, correct?"

"Yes, but—"

"And you paid Sukey for her services, did you not?"

"That's not—"

"And then you set the woman up in a love nest in Kensington, is that right?"

"But—"

"But nothing! The woman is your mistress, dash it, and that makes her ineligible to be your bride."

"Not if I love her, it does not."

"Deuce take it, you can love a woman without marrying her. Men do it all the time. In fact, I'd wager more men love their mistresses than love their wives."

"I could not dishonor the woman I love that way. I thought you would understand about honor, but I was wrong. It is love you do not understand. You are our father's son after all, no matter how much you kick over the traces."

"Blast it, do not speak to me of the earl. He wants power and prestige. I only want you to be happy. All this talk of love and honor is for mooncalves. You are still bedding the girl, aren't you?"

So now Ty had a black eye to match his black armband.

Chapter 22

$\mathcal{H}$ is sister did not hit him. Ann was a lady, the Duchess of Illington. She poured scalding hot tea in his lap, instead.

"How could you, you dolt? I expected better of you, the heir to the earldom, a war hero, a leader of men. Hah!"

So Ann had read the announcement, too. Ty mopped at his pantaloons, wishing Mindle or Winsted were in Town to see about his wardrobe, instead of that old stick at St. Ives House. He did the best he could, then said, "I am trying to dissuade Nonny against this disastrous alliance."

"What, with your fists?" Ann shook her head. "If that is not just like a man. I am not, however, speaking of Nonny's calf love."

She had read both announcements. He sighed. "My marriage was a matter of honor. A debt of obligation."

"I never assumed anything else, you gudgeon. What, Tyverne the True acting the cad? I will believe that when the cows come home. Whatever reasons you had for marrying this unfortunate Miss Gannon must have been good ones. There are no explanations on earth good enough, though, for not inviting your own and only sister to the wedding!"

"There was no ti—" he began.

"That I should have to read it in the newspapers? Be

quizzed by every gossip in Town without knowing what
you wished me to say?"

"I did write to you."

She waved his own letter under his nose. "After the
fact, and only because you wanted something. And that
is another thing, you great ox. How could you think I
would refuse to have my niece here? That you would so
much as doubt your daughter's welcome in my home is
an insult, sirrah, and I am glad Nonny darkened your
daylights for you!"

"Boxing cant, Your Grace? Perhaps I ought to reconsider bringing Melinda here after all." He knew enough
to duck the pillow she tossed his way.

"And worst of all"—Ann had the St. Ives nose, too—
"how could you possibly leave a child, a tiny, fragile
infant at that, with a . . . a pig farmer? If you had not
returned today, I was going to fetch her myself, with a
nurse and a maid and a respectable wet nurse."

"I take it, then, that the infant and her attendants will
be greeted favorably." He studied the wet spot on his
pants. "Does that, um, include Miss Croft?"

"The young woman in the letter?" Ann knew precisely
whom he meant, having read the missive ten times, but
she could not resist making her stiff-rumped eldest
brother squirm. She was intrigued to see a flush creep
up his cheeks. Definitely the young woman in the letter.
"I see no reason for you to think I suddenly need a
companion," she began, just to tease him further. "It is
not as if I am in my dotage, you know. I am still years
younger than you. Just how old is this Miss Croft?"

Now the viscount examined his boots for scratches.
"Um, the perfect age," he mumbled into his collar.

So there was hope for Tyverne yet, his sister was delighted to see. "Well, I suppose we might see if we suit."

"You will. You have to. She is . . ."

"Perfect?"

Now he grinned, relieved to have Ann's approval. "Almost. She has this little space between her teeth—"

"Save me the rhapsodizing, brother. I got enough of it from Nonny about his Miss Dunsley." She poured him out another cup of tea, with nary a drop going amiss this time. "Just tell me when to expect them."

"As soon as I resolve a few matters here in Town. But don't you need to confer with the duke before bringing an entire entourage into his home?"

"Illington will not care. I doubt if he would even notice, he is here so seldom," Ann said in bitter tones.

"I, ah, I am sorry."

"Do not be. We both prefer it this way. He is off at some house party or other with his cronies and their inamoratas, even though the physicians warned Illington that such drinking and whoring will kill him. I am content to stay in London with the theater and the libraries, the balls and my charity work."

That sounded dismal to Ty, very similar to his parents' marriage, except Lady Stivern had managed to present the earl with tokens of whatever affection they shared on at least four occasions. "What about children?" the viscount asked. "I know you always wanted a houseful."

The duchess busied herself, straightening the sugar cubes in their dish. "His Grace's first wife never conceived after their daughter, nor any of his mistresses, it seems. He gave up after two years or so of our marriage, to my relief. So you can see why I am so eager to have your daughter come to stay." She swiftly changed the subject: "So what are you going to do about Nonny?"

Ty relaxed against the cushions. "Lud, there is not much I can do, short of tying the nodcock up for a year or two. I thought I might try buying the woman off. I'll need to see my man of affairs first, to find out what a third son is worth to a fortune hunter."

"But what if she is not an adventuress? And how sad for Nonny if she is, and he truly loves her."

Ty sat up again, not comfortable with talk of true love. "How am I to know?" he asked, not sure which question he was asking.

Ann was no help to him either way. "How am I supposed to know? I was married to Illington straight out of the schoolroom, nearly.''

"Yes, but since? I know you have a court of admirers.'' Ann was a deuced handsome woman, Ty recognized, even if she was his sister. She was tall like the St. Ives men, but instead of their breadth and bulk she had a full, lush figure, thank goodness, and dressed in the height of fashion. The devil, he thought, the Duchess of Illington must set the style. She had the same gold hair as her brothers, piled now in some intricate arrangement atop her head, and the same blue eyes. Aside from her beauty and her intelligence, the duchess had an air of regality about her, an elegance men would prize to have at their sides. To say nothing of her generous charms in their beds. "Surely one of your cicisbeos . . . ?''

Now she did hit him. "I spoke my marriage vows the same as you did, brother. Women understand honor, too.''

Ty went to his club that evening. Not Brooks's or Watier's, where he knew he would be the main course in the dining room and the joker in the card room and the footnote in the reading room. No, he went to Gilson's, a small place where military men gathered to discuss the war—not women, weddings, or who was tupping whose wife. No one there offered congratulations or condolences. No one mentioned his brother, his baby daughter, or his black eye, thank goodness. Instead they conducted serious business, soldiers' business, mapping the course of the Peninsular Campaign on a chart on the wall, with pins and flags and scraps of paper.

The other men, retired officers, mostly, but some serving soldiers home on sick leave or army business, wanted to know what news Major Tyverne had.

The war could have moved to Mongolia for all Ty knew. Or for all he cared tonight. Suddenly the very foundation of his life was turning to quicksand, and he did not know where to find solid ground. He settled in a comfortable leather chair in the corner with a bottle of cognac and a glass, letting the battle talk wash over him while he contemplated life, death, and a pair of green eyes.

Considering that poets and philosophers had been cogitating for centuries on the same questions—except for the green eyes, of course—Ty was not surprised he had not come to a conclusion after three hours and half the bottle had disappeared. After the other half, the viscount considered, perhaps he would no longer care that he was drowning in a sea of confusion.

He never got to find out, for a recent arrival at the club was full of news, not of a new offensive against the French, but of a duel outside a gaming hell. Stupid civilians, the old campaigners said, shaking their heads, wasting lives over trivia when the future of the Empire was at stake. Foolish hotheads would do better, they said, to join the army and shoot Frenchmen, instead of each other.

Ty agreed wholeheartedly, especially when he learned that one of the fools, one of the cloth-headed duelists, was his own little brother. The clunch, it seemed, had taken on one Finster Dunsley, a loose screw for sure. Both men were wounded, the captain reported, although St. Ives was expected to recover.

Killing one's future in-laws was not the way to embark on married life, Ty hazily decided as he raced home, no matter how deserving. Worse, dueling was illegal. If Dunsley died, Nonny would have to flee the country, or hang. Worst of all in Lord Tyverne's inebriated opinion, Nonny might expire before he could strangle him.

On the brighter side, maybe Nonny would see what kind of family he was aligning himself with, what kind of future he would have with Miss Dunsley. If he had to defend her honor at every turn, he'd never turn five-and-twenty.

By the time he arrived back at St. Ives House, Ty was nearly sober, and the surgeon had come and gone. The bewigged butler's nose was so out of joint he could have smelled his own ear. Ty did not stop to listen to Gilbert's complaints but took the steps three at a time to his brother's room.

The bullet had passed cleanly through the younger man's leg, Ty was glad to hear from Nonny's valet, who instantly resigned now that Lord Tyverne had returned. Mopping up blood was not what he was hired to do, the man announced as he left. Nor was he going to follow his master to Botany Bay.

Nonny's cheek felt warm to Ty's touch, but he roused from his drugged state to smile at his brother. "Knew you would come. Tyverne the True, we always called you."

"Go to sleep, cawker. We'll get you out of this coil."

Missing his man Winsted more than he thought possible, Ty sent a footman to find Dunsley's condition if he could, and another to the mews, to have a coach and team made ready. The way he saw it, he had to get Nonny out of London before daybreak when the magistrates would have men knocking on the door. If Dunsley died, Ty could ship Nonny to their brother in the Americas, even if he had to send him halfway around the world to avoid the blockades. If the dirty dish lived, the contretemps would be forgotten in time and no harm done— except for the new gray hairs Viscount Tyverne was bound to develop overnight.

Meanwhile, while they waited to see his opponent's fate, Nonny needed care. The frightened footmen were going to be no help, nor the disapproving Gilbert. Winsted, though, knew more about gunshots than a hundred surgeons, and old Mags had an entire herbal arsenal against fevers. Ty could take him to Kent. To Delia. Tonight.

As luck would have it, Nonny woke up while Ty was trying to drape his greatcoat around him, before carrying him down to the carriage. The viscount was not about to entrust his brother to the weak-kneed footmen, despite his own bad arm.

Young St. Ives refused to go. "Not without Thea."

"Impossible," Ty told him, buttoning the coat. "I cannot bring a woman of that ilk to Miss Croft's."

"Thea's not what you think. You have to listen."

"I will listen in the carriage."

"No. You'll never send for her, then. I know you. You are just like our father. Your mind is made up, and you will do things your own way, saying you know best. Well, not this time, you don't, if you will not even hear me out." He shoved Ty's arm aside. "If you will not fetch Thea, leave me here."

"Don't be a fool. You might have to leave the country."

"I go with her or not at all. Go on, leave me here to die. I would not wish to live without her anyway, but you could never understand that, could you?"

Ty could haul his brother down the stairs, for Nonny was too weak to put up much of a fight, or he could dose him with more laudanum and wait for him to fall asleep again. Or he could listen.

So he heard how Miss Dunsley was raised as a well-bred young female, daughter to a schoolteacher and a music instructor in Norwich. When both of her parents died recently, she was given into the care of her scapegrace uncle, a Captain Sharp. Dunsley had tried to make her into a dealer for his card games, games he would rig to win with her assistance. Thea refused, and refused, also, to accept the advances of Finster Dunsley's cronies, for his profit.

So he drugged her and sold her to Sukey Johnson, a madam notorious for luring green girls off incoming mail coaches with the promise of work. Sukey's clientele never minded; a virgin was a virgin, willing or not.

Nonny and some of his friends happened to stop by Sukey's that night, and he saw Thea, painted and primped and half asleep.

"I chose her because she was so pretty, and so sad. I thought . . . I thought I could make things easier for her, if I was her first. But then she started weeping."

Ty sighed. "You should have left right then. Hell, you should not have been there in the first place."

"I couldn't leave. Thea did not want to become a prostitute. She is a good girl, I swear. So I gave Ma Johnson what she'd paid Finster Dunsley for Thea, and more besides, and took Thea away. I couldn't bring her here. You have seen Gilbert the Gargoyle. And I could not take her to Father in Warwickshire."

"Hell, no."

So St. Ives borrowed a friend's rooms in Kensington and installed her there. They talked, they shared a meal, they fell in love. But there was talk, a lot of talk, more than Nonny could tolerate, about the woman he loved. He could not afford a special license, and he had promised Ty not to elope to Gretna, so he did the next best thing: He announced their engagement.

"Then Dunsley decided I ought to pay him for his niece. Else he'd go to the earl. What else could I do but challenge him to a duel?"

"You could have shot the bastard in cold blood. The world would have been a better place."

Chapter 23

Ty sent a message back to the St. Ives stables to bring out the big traveling coach instead of the lighter, faster vehicle he'd been planning on taking. Now he needed a driver and a groom. He already had a tiger, it seemed, for Dover refused to be left behind. The boy was not going to stay on in London with grudge-faced Gilbert, even if he had to ride on top of the carriage. School could wait, a grinning Dover told his idol, the longer the better. Miss Dilly needed the extra help. The dog could ride in the boot.

Ty made sure there was room for both inside the carriage, of course. Until he had to make space for his sister, her dresser, and half her belongings, it seemed, for Her Grace refused to be left behind, either.

"What about your reputation?" Ty protested when the duchess arrived at his doorstep in response to the note he'd sent. "I would not have my sister's name dragged through the muck along with Miss Dunsley's."

"Gammon. It is my reputation that is going to see all of us through this. If Nonny truly intends to wed the girl, then they need my approval. Who is going to refuse to recognize the Duchess of Illington's sister-in-law? No one who wants an invitation to my parties, for certain."

"Yes, but we have only Nonny's word that the chit is respectable, that she is not what she seems."

Ann straightened her fur cape. "Since when is one of my brothers' words not good enough for me?"

So they went in the duke's huge, lumbering state carriage, with the St. Ives coach following, and another for baggage. The heavier carriage was better for Nonny, anyway, so he would not be as jostled on the journey, although it might add hours to the trip. Ty regretted he could not simply whisk his brother off and be with Delia posthaste. The duchess regretted she had not had time to find a respectable wet nurse. Nonny regretted he was too battered to go knock on Miss Dunsley's door and explain matters.

The job fell to Ty. He regretted that most of all.

Miss Dunsley was a dark-haired girl, dressed in a plain, modest gown that was obviously home-sewn. She had a sweet, heart-shaped face, a nicely rounded shape, a polite manner, and an educated accent. Despite her shabby surroundings, she appeared ladylike, Ty was glad to see. She also, unfortunately, had a lady's sensibilities. She saw her beloved's brother and feared the worst. Her dear Agamemnon was dead, killed in her defense. She fainted.

Ty caught her before she hit her head on the floor, wrenching his wounded arm. Now what? Deuce take it, Delia would never faint when a fellow needed to be on the road. A regular trooper was Miss Croft. A regular pain in the . . . shoulder was Miss Dunsley, as Ty slung her across his neck and half flung her into the carriage with his sister and brother.

"Damn you to hell, Tyverne, what have you done to her?" Nonny demanded, while Ann reached for her vinaigrette, saying, "You always did have a way with women, brother."

After sending Ann's abigail back to gather Miss Dunsley's few belongings, Ty decided to ride up with the driver.

Now his cavalcade was complete. Besides Dover and the dog, the viscount had Miss Dunsley, the duchess, and his dunderhead brother in tow. An entire marching column would have been less noticeable departing town, he swore. Next he'd have a detachment from the sheriff's office on his trail. But he was headed in the right direction, back to Delia.

After what seemed like a hundred stops—Miss Dunsley suffered motion sickness, besides a crisis of nerves— Ty hired a horse at one of the inns and rode ahead, now that dawn was lightening the sky. He needed to get to Faircroft House first, to prepare Miss Croft for the onslaught of strangers. He could stay at the inn, but he did not want to have his brother in such a public place, if Miss Dunsley's uncle cocked up his toes. Nonny thought he'd struck Finster's head with his pistol shot—damn if Ty wouldn't have to teach his brother better aim—but head wounds bled a lot, so there was no telling the cur's condition.

Ty would have to go back to London himself to find out soon, because he could not trust that stick of a butler to play the spy. He had to transfer funds, also, and check the income on that place he owned in Yorkshire. The unentailed property might do for Nonny and his ninnyhammer of a fiancée if her uncle lived, rather than having them emigrate. Then, too, if the scoundrel survived, Ty meant to make him sorry for the fact. No one, not the prime minister nor the man in the moon, got to injure Tyverne's brother and get away with a minor scratch. Nonny was family, and Ty looked after his own.

He wished he had his own horse right now. Diablo would have had him at Delia's doorstep in jig time. This tired old nag could barely outdistance the caravan of coaches, much less take the fences and walls that stood on the cross-country route if Ty left the road. Thunderation, Ty had to admit as he urged the beast to exert itself a bit more, it was not Diablo he missed. It was Delia.

Delia was done with her ride for the day. She went out early, when the day was waking up, when the birds were beginning to call, when no one was abroad to notice the breeches she wore under her green riding habit. She loved the feel of a strong horse under her, flying with the wind. For so long she had been plodding through the maze of her dilemmas, her feet too firmly on the ground. Now Delia was lighter, freer. Now she could soar again. Baby Melinda was thriving, and they were all going to London together.

Clarence and Gwen warned her not to get her hopes up. A gentleman's promises were easily made, more easily forgotten, they said. She could still accept Dallsworth, they told her, for that bird in the hand was a ring on her finger. Tyverne's offer was for a visit, a possible position with his sister, a glorified maid to the child.

But they did not know about the kiss. A man of honor like the viscount did not make idle promises, and did not go back on his word. More importantly, he did not toss kisses around like coins. Delia knew that in her heart, where she cherished the memory, and hoped for the future. He would be back in a week or less. He'd said so. His kiss confirmed it.

She walked out of the stable, into the daylight, and saw a horse approaching. Her eyes took a moment to adjust to the brighter light, but then she recognized the uniformed rider's gold hair and broad shoulders. Almost as if Delia had conjured him out of her daydreams, Lord Tyverne brought his horse to a halt and dismounted.

Conscious of Jed, her stable man, coming to lead the horse away, Delia merely smiled and welcomed him back. He looked tired and . . . bruised. Her smile faded.

"The babe?" he asked first, taking the hand she offered.

Delia thought he would shake her hand, or kiss her fingers. He held it as they walked around the stable toward the front of the house.

"Does fine. And you, my lord? Did your business go well?"

"About as well as a three-legged dog does, chasing rabbits."

Delia wanted to brush the hair back from his forehead,

or gently touch the discoloration around his eye, but they were in full view of the house now, and he still held her hand. "Can you tell me about it?"

"I am afraid I have to do more than tell you; I have to beg a favor of you. Deuce take it, every time I seem to have paid my debt to your family, I find myself needing yet another boon."

"Friends do not keep score, you know, marking favors in debit or credit columns to be repaid."

He squeezed her hand, coming to a halt. "We are friends, are we not?"

"I like to think so, my lord."

"And I like my friends to call me Ty."

Delia nodded. "My friends call me Dilly."

"Delia is prettier. But I suppose I have put my request off long enough." He set out again, then slowed his steps to match her shorter ones. "You see, my brother shot a man last night. Lud, was it only last night? It feels like a month."

Delia could not help the gasp that escaped her.

"No, Nonny is not a cold-blooded murderer. The dastard he shot deserved it, and the thing was a duel, with seconds and witnesses, but his opponent might die for all that. Nonny is wounded, and I need to hide him away until we find out if charges will be pressed against him, or if I have to smuggle him out of the country."

"And you wish to hide him here, at Faircroft?"

"Between Mags and Mindle and my man Winsted, and you, of course, I know he would get excellent care, without drawing the attention he would at the inn. No one will think anything of my coming to Kent to make arrangements for the child or visiting her here."

"Very well. The other servants will have to know, though—Cook if she is to prepare invalid foods, the maids who will change the linens, but they are good girls. They will not speak of your brother if I ask them not to."

"You do understand that he might be considered a criminal?"

"The man he shot was a villain, wasn't he?"

"The man he shot sold his own niece into a house of prostitution."

"Your brother will be welcome."

Now Ty did bring her hand to his mouth for a kiss. "No matter what you say, I am in your debt. The coach is on its way, but there is worse. There always is, it seems. I had to bring Nonny's sweetheart along. He would not leave London without her, much less the country."

"The woman you thought was such a misalliance?"

He nodded. "Miss Thea Dunsley, late of Sukey Johnson's bordello. She seems a pleasant enough widgeon whose reputation was destroyed through no fault of her own. The *ton* won't care. They will accuse you of harboring a fallen woman."

"You forget that I took in Belinda. And a wounded soldier. How much smokier can my reputation get with a murderer and his mistress?"

"I knew you were trumps," he said with one of his rare smiles. "But there's more, the worst part. My sister is also on her way."

"The duchess?" Delia squeaked, ready to rush into the house to change her dress, dust the furniture, help Cook bake a fresh cake.

"Her Grace, herself. She is an interfering, managing female who will be in your hair constantly. She wants the baby, you see."

"My baby? Ah, your baby, Melly?"

"Melinda, yes. My sister has no children of her own, which situation does not seem likely to change. She would be a good mother, I think."

"Despite being interfering and managing?"

"Because of that. She would not relegate the infant to a forgotten nursery with the servants. Melinda would have the best of everything."

"And a duke for a father."

"Not precisely, but that's all to the good, with this duke."

Delia reclaimed her hand. "I see." And she did. There was no place for her. "Well, I suppose Her Grace will be welcome also, to grow accustomed to Melly."

"Thank you. That's what I thought, but I have made no decisions yet. Nonny and Miss Dunsley mentioned that they would be happy to begin married life with a daughter. Thea says she adores infants. Her neighbors, it appears, had a large family, and she helped care for the youngest ones. If she and my brother emigrate to the Americas, or even relocate to Yorkshire, there would never be any gossip about Melinda's birth. She would not even have to change her name, and I would make sure she wanted for nothing."

"So far away," Delia spoke her thoughts aloud.

"And far away from being labeled a bastard. Still, there is no hurry to decide, not until this latest hobble of Nonny's is resolved."

"Do you mean to permit St. Ives and Miss Dunsley to marry, then? I thought you were so opposed to the unequal match."

"The choice is not mine to make, as both my brother and sister reminded me. I confess, I am hoping that if Nonny and his lady see more of each other here while he recuperates, they might reconsider. My brother was never a good patient."

"But a good boxer, I think."

Ty touched the tender skin around his eye. "I taught him well."

They were almost at the front door, and Delia had a million things to do, to get ready for her guests, but she was curious. "If your brother and Miss Dunsley do not reconsider, what will you do?"

"I suppose I shall have to purchase another special license for them when he recovers, or see them to Gretna. Both of them are underage, and my father will never give his permission. Miss Dunsley's guardian will not be in condition to give his."

"So you will let them have their inconvenient love

match, despite all the drawbacks and your own disbelief in its existence?"

"I am not my father."

"I do not understand," Delia said.

"Neither do I, but I am trying to learn."

Chapter 24

*L*earning was good. Delia was learning that air castles did not always collapse all at once. Sometimes they shrank and shriveled until only a pretty husk of a rainbow fantasy was left. Lord Tyverne spoke again of his debt to her, pressed her hand, then rode to meet his oncoming party. That was the last she had spoken privately with him for days. He never sought her company, never took her aside, never invited her to go with him when he drove to Canterbury or Dover. Now that his sister was here, Delia supposed, Ty could recall how a real lady behaved. With one brother embroiled in an unsuitable affair, he would not wish to entangle himself, the heir, with another mere nobody. Another mere air brick fell to the ground.

She was too busy to suffer the megrims over some muddleheaded military gentleman, Delia told herself. The first thing she did, after sending Dover to find old Mags and getting the new invalid settled under Mindle's care, was introduce her lady guests to Melinda.

The baby was growing by the minute. One could almost see her cheeks filling out, and her belly expand with each feeding. She was starting to accept some of the goat's milk, without developing the colic, which Mags said was a good sign and meant they could soon dispense with Hester Wigmore. The baby did not seem to care who held her, almost as if she knew that, without a mother of her own, she had to gather affection from everyone. Melinda turned her face in to nurse from Delia, Thea, and the duchess, all of whom were equally as entranced by her, and argued over whose turn it was to offer the warmed milk bottle. She had so much attention, in fact, that no one bothered to shoo the dog out of the cradle anymore.

Either of her guests, Delia decided, would make little Melly a fine mother, although the duchess could offer more worldly advantages, of course. Her Grace was a charming young woman, near in age to Delia, stunning in her looks and gowns and diamonds, but not nearly as full of her own consequence as Delia had feared. She offered to sort Aunt Eliza's yarns, and endeared herself to Nanny by admiring the infant. By that first afternoon, she and Delia were the best of friends.

"So please stop all that Your Grace nonsense," Ann said. "If you cannot bring yourself to use my given name, then call me Duchy, the way Nonny does. Ty hates it, of course."

"Of course he does. It's degrading," she said with a laugh as the two novices tried to change Melinda's nappy, which was most definitely beneath a duchess's dignity. "You can call me Dilly. Everyone does, and Lord—Ty hates that, too."

"Which makes it better." Ann giggled in a very unduchess-like manner. "Oh, I knew I was going to like you."

Delia and Miss Dunsley were quickly on a first-name basis also. Thea was so innocent and gentle, Delia could not understand how any man could think her Haymarket ware. Thea was so sweet, Delia could see how any man would wish to protect the younger girl, shelter her from the evils of the world, love her.

Mr. St. Ives did love her, that was obvious. Once he was out of danger from the fever, and free from the pain and the laudanum, he was never content unless Thea was in sight. So they let him hold the baby, too.

Nonny, as the honorable Agamemnon insisted, was almost as handsome as his brother. He was neither as large

nor as well-muscled, but he had a ready smile and an
ease of manner foreign to Ty's nature. He laughed when
Melinda grasped his finger in her tiny ones, and cradled
her in his arms when she slept, while the women sat at
his bedside with their sewing. Melinda was going to have
enough baby caps and gowns and blankets for five
children.

Thea and Nonny might have those four others; Ann
never would. Who then should have the baby? Delia
wondered, wisely ignoring the wrench at her heart that
she could not be in the contest. With Nonny and Thea,
the baby would have a fresh start, and a loving father.

"Just look at that," Nonny was saying as the infant
puckered up her face in complaint that her next meal
was not ready. "A true St. Ives. You look just like the
earl with that sour expression, my little dove. No one
would take you for anything else."

When Nonny was more fit, they gathered in the parlor
in the evenings, where Thea played the pianoforte for
them, better than Delia ever could, and the others listened or sang along or played whist, to Aunt Eliza's de-
light. Lord Tyverne joined them, but stayed with the
company, never asking Delia to step apart. Delia was not
quite as delighted.

The first thing Ty did after getting Nonny settled with
Winsted and Mags arguing over his medicines, was to go
and see about his horse. Not the hayburner he had so
recently ridden, but his own horse, Diablo. The devil was
the only one who had time for him, it seemed. Delia had
disappeared in a flurry of petticoats, and his sister hardly
left the nursery. She was content to watch the child for
hours, although Ty could not see where Melinda had
many accomplishments in her repertoire. Miss Dunsley
had even less to say.

The chit was afraid of him, likely knowing he could
send her back to London or put her on a boat to India
if he wished. His very size likely terrorized her, Ty reck-
oned, and his brusque manner, too, damn him for a

rough old warrior. Ty had no way of reassuring her except staying out of her presence.

He had to stay away from Delia, too. Not that she had ever shown the least fear of him or his bellowing, but that gleam in his sister's eye boded ill for any plans he might have. It would be just like Ann to stick her long nose where it was least wanted. If he took Delia away with him, Ann was liable to say he'd compromised Miss Croft, and demand he marry her. He did not want his hand forced, and Zeus, he did not want Delia forced into a marriage of convenience that she would abhor.

Perhaps he had read more in that tender kiss than she had intended, anyway. Delia was a generous, caring woman; just see the way she had taken in his family. What if she treated him as she would any other needy, wounded creature? She might not be interested in him at all. Gads, what if he pressed his unwanted attentions on her? What a horrid way to repay her kindness.

There was nothing for it but for Ty to stay away from her until the matter with his brother was resolved, his sister was back in London, and his own impulses were under control. When he was near Delia, his good manners and his good intentions all took wing. He knew he was just as liable to sweep her into his arms as pass her the salt at supper. Toss her over his shoulder rather than toss her a discard at whist. Unbraid her fiery hair and comb it through his fingers instead of singing a chorus.

Taking tea with her was torture. A walk would have been worse. Sitting next to Delia in the carriage, her thigh pressed against his? That would have been hardest of all. Speaking of which, he was sick of those cursed cold baths.

So he rode his horse, always enough of a challenge to keep a man from daydreaming. Either you were on your toes around Diablo, or you were on your rump. The gelding was not as fresh as he'd expected, so the Faircroft groom was still doing a decent job, whoever the chap was. Ty supposed he'd get the bill eventually for hats and boots, if not for a surgeon's stitches.

His first stop was at Gwen, Lady Croft's father's home, where Sir Clarence and she resided with their three hellion-by-hearsay children. The house was cold, the butler was colder. He gave Grim Gilbert competition in the peevish stakes, but he did show Major Tyverne into the library, where Delia's cousin was napping with a newspaper over his head, or else he was hiding from his wife, children, and crotchety father-in-law.

Ty invited him to take the entire family to London, if he wished, to stay at St. Ives House. He explained how his sister had come with a young lady friend and their maid to visit the baby, and so Ty needed to beg the use of the Crofts' new inheritance a bit longer. He and his man were staying at the inn, of course, so there was no hint of impropriety, he reassured the priggish popinjay in his puce waistcoat and pomaded hair. There was also no hint of his brother in the viscount's explanation.

Ty wanted the baronet and his brood out of town. He did not want them underfoot, with a duchess at their own doorstep, and he did not want them discovering, then broadcasting to the corners of Kent, that they had two sons of an earl visiting. Nor did he want them nattering at Delia about Dallsworth. So he made the offer of his family's town house irresistible to the greedy pair, throwing in the use of the St. Ives theater box, the St. Ives carriages, and the St. Ives accounts at London's finest furniture manufacturers and upholsterers.

Gwen could do her own shopping, Nonny's presence could remain quiet, and Gilbert the butler could go hang. He deserved nothing less for showing such blatant disapproval of his employers. Granted Stivern paid his salary, but the bilious butler'd had an easy time of it all these years, with the earl so seldom in Town. If Gilbert quit now, rather than serve this clump of toadstools, good riddance. Ty had a mind to offer the position to Mindle when—not if—Delia came to Town. Who else would play backgammon and piquet with Aunt Eliza? The ex-valet and the excitable spinster were old friends, if nothing more.

Another pair of old friends were reunited that week. When Ty rode into Canterbury to see about obtaining another special license, Stephen Anselm insisted on riding back with him to visit the duchess. He remembered the former Lady Ann fondly from school holidays spent with Ty, the vicar said, and wished to pay his respects.

If the reunion appeared a bit fonder, and a tad less respectful than Ty expected, he shrugged it off. Anselm was a born flirt, that was all. He had Delia laughing, the dastard, and Thea blushing. Deuce take it if even the infant did not stare up at him, fascinated by the gold rims of his spectacles. Rather than watch his old friend pour the butter boat over Ann next, Ty went for another ride.

This time he visited Belinda's father, Squire Gannon. The squire's lands appeared well tended and prosperous, at least. The old fool might be a dreadful parent, but he was a decent agriculturist. It remained to be seen if he was a dutiful magistrate.

After asking about the infant's welfare, Gannon slapped his beefy thigh and laughed. "Give you the guardianship of a slip of a girl? Do not be absurd. Gals have guardians to protect them from such as you."

At least the man had some scruples, Ty was happy to see, although he had to put a check on his temper at the slur to his integrity. "The young lady is currently here in your territory under the protection of my sister, the Duchess of Illington. I merely wish the formal, legal guardianship."

"The chit is, what, seventeen to your nine and twenty? And no relationship? Not bloody likely."

"Very well, then, you become Miss Dunsley's guardian until she marries my brother." Ty saw no reason to mention that his brother was also in Kent, and every reason not to, if Gannon were a conscientious upholder of the law.

Gannon scowled. "Why would I want to do a daft thing like that? Young misses are the devil's own handmaidens. And deuced expensive, too boot."

"You would have no expenses, I swear, and little enough to do with the girl. You never need meet her, if you wish. Miss Dunsley does, however, need an official guardian. Her current one, her uncle, tried to sell her into prostitution."

"Hellfire."

Ty nodded his agreement. "Not hot enough for the dastard."

"Still, the fellow is her uncle."

"Who can come back and legally claim her at any moment." Until Ty shot him, if Finster Dunsley were not already dead. "But come, you lost your own daughter to greed and foolishness. Have you learned nothing from your mistakes?"

"Here now, my gel's got nothing to do with this." Gannon took out a large square of linen and wiped at his eyes. "Demme if I don't miss the chit more every day."

"No, Belinda has nothing to do with Dunsley, except that now you have the power to rescue some other poor innocent child from so dire a fate."

A crafty look came over Gannon's suddenly dry eyes. "Aye, but why should I do you any favors, my lord?"

"Some men set great store in their grandchildren. You did express a wish to see Melinda, did you not?"

"What I want is to bring her here where she belongs, but, yes, I would like to see the chit. See if there is any of my gel in the mite."

"She is beautiful, like her mother. And Miss Dunsley is helping to care for her. You can visit with both of them at the same time when you put your seal on the papers my man Macurdle is drawing up. Shall I send for you when the documents arrive?"

Gannon took his time answering. "I suppose."

Ty stood to leave. He waved his arm around, indicating the farms and fields, the house and barns. "You know, you have no one else to leave this to, what you have worked so hard for your entire life long. You leave the land in trust for Melinda, for her sons, and I will match its value in the same account. You won't be able to touch it, but your blood kin will still work this land when you are gone. That's something."

Ty left the man wiping his eyes again, thinking of those great-grandsons he'd likely never see. Ty was thinking of his own lands, his own patrimony, his own sons. He urged Diablo faster.

Chapter 25

*H*e was going to do it. No more agonizing, no more delays, no more worrying about mourning, Miss Croft's emotions, or his sister's machinations. Delia had returned his kiss, he knew it, just as he knew she must have felt the joyful chorus singing through his soul. She did not kiss other men that way, by Heaven, or they'd be lined up in her entryway, panting. No man with a dram of blood coursing in his veins would walk away from a woman who kissed him like that.

As for Ann, Anselm had taken the duchess into Canterbury to visit the cathedral today. She'd left her maid behind to chaperone Thea and Nonny, but answered Ty's raised eyebrow with a laugh. She was a securely married woman, Her Grace had said, and Anselm was her spiritual advisor. Besides, it was an open carriage, and they would be back before nightfall.

As for leaving their brother and his fiancée under such haphazard supervision, Ann had laughed again, citing Aunt Eliza, Nanny, Baby Melinda, and Delia in and out of the sickroom. The duchess added that if the pair were seriously considering marriage, better they get to know each other first. Ty had to agree.

He had to get on with his own courting, too. The viscount thought he knew Miss Croft well enough by now to get the job done right this time. He tried different words out in rehearsal, watching Diablo's ears for reaction. He was amazed to think how hard he'd struggled to find the correct phrases the other times, when the outcome did not matter. Now, he feared, it was a matter of life and death.

"Dedication?"

"Devotion?"

"Desire?"

The gelding's ears pricked forward at the last, but that may have been because a creature rustled in the hedgerow alongside the road. No, desire would never do. Miss Croft was a gently bred female. A man did not mention his burning, rampantly lustful yearnings for a lady, not unless he wanted her to run away screaming or, worse, crying. Zeus, she could even faint.

Devotion was a good word, Ty decided, wishing he had a pencil to write it down. Thunderation, he wished he had a ring to give Delia. The one he'd placed by Belinda's hand was gold, a wedding band. Ty wanted an engagement ring this time, something that sparkled, to remind Delia every time she saw it that he would wait as long as necessary, until a respectable mourning period was over, or until he sold his commission, if she insisted. She ought to have rubies to go with her hair, he considered, or emeralds to match her eyes. Surely there was a jeweler in Dover, or Canterbury, where they must hold a million weddings. Or he could wait until he returned to London and buy her something special.

No, Ty was not going to put the proposal off. Who knew when he could bring his courage to the sticking point again? Diablo snorted. There was no rabbit in the hedgerow this time.

Well, if he had no ring, and deuced few words, he ought to have flowers. Delia seemed to set great store in the things, filling the house with them for Belinda's wedding, and then her funeral. He was riding right past the gates to Dallsworth's place, Ty knew, and could beg a nosegay from the baron's greenhouses, he supposed, right after Hell froze over and the devil put on ice skates.

He slowed the gelding to peer at the weeds at the verge of the road. It was nearly spring; surely something was blooming.

At last Ty's patience was rewarded with a narrow clump of tiny purple somethings—he knew they were not violets—peeping out of dark green leaves. He dismounted and picked a handful, then the remaining two or three when Diablo ate his first bouquet. A battered soldier, a few measly sprigs, no ring—a fine bargain he was offering his would-be bride.

The deal deteriorated. The person who managed Diablo was not around, Jed Groom told Ty as he backed away from Diablo's teeth, hooves, and anything else that moved. By the time the viscount was done seeing to his horse, the weeds were limp in his hand and he himself stank of horse and sweat. He'd have to wait, after all.

But there was Delia, out walking her dog in the grass at the front of the house. The yipping mutt was his dog, dash it, and that was another reason for getting married, so he could say the fluffy little mongrel was his wife's pet, instead of having to admit ownership. His wife. Now there was a good word, Ty thought, forgetting his previous antipathy for the noxious noun.

"My wife?" he mumbled to himself as he walked closer to Delia and the dog.

Delia looked up and smiled.

He was lost. He handed her the flowers, sank onto one knee in front of her—that's how a fellow did the thing, wasn't it?—and said, "My wife?"

She laughed at him.

Delia had seen the viscount ride toward the stables, so she drew Angelina in that direction. If he headed back toward the inn without coming into the house, if he gave her the merest nod before walking politely past her to go visit his brother, then she would know once and for all, and could stop hoping.

He strode straight toward her. Delia's heart sped up and she smiled. He held out a clump of . . . dead weeds? . . . and her heart took off and she grinned. Then, with a pained expression on his face, as if he had eaten something rancid, Ty spit out what had to be the briefest proposal in history, and her heart soared, but she giggled. She looked down to gain her composure and, despite her best intentions, laughed outright. Her handsome swain, her knight in white horse hairs, had knelt in the reason she was walking Angelina.

Without a sound other than the dog's yips and Miss Croft's chuckles, Ty got up, did an about-face, a scarlet face at that, and marched back to the inn.

Aunt Rosalie arrived before Delia could walk into the village to apologize. "Such tales, my girl," the dowager Lady Presmacott began as soon as her footman put down the carriage steps. "Clarence always was a talebearer, but the newspapers and scandal sheets are all full of the goings on here, so I had to come see for myself. Duels and dead demireps, hurried weddings and who knows what else? Besides, with Clarence and Gwen in town, I thought it best to leave rather than have to claim 'em as kin. That widgeon Gwen thought I'd spend my time showing her the best shops. And Clarence is growing fat as a flawn. So tell me, what is this about Stivern's heir courting you, then that peagoose Belinda, then you again? I could make neither heads nor tales from Clarence's blather. And wipe that silly grin off your face, miss. With your freckles and hair, it makes you look like a clown at Astley's Amphitheater. And what is that sack you have on? I swear, it's no wonder the man left if that's the best you can do. Clarence says you whistled away a fortune here in Hillsdale, besides. Such idiocy must have come from the Linbury side, along with that dreadful hair, and is that watering pot Linbury aunt of yours still battening on your generosity? And why have you not offered tea yet, nor shown me the infant? If it looks like George, we are all sunk. Why ain't you wearing a bonnet, Dilly? If you are determined to lead apes in Hell, you ought to put on caps. And where is my maid? I need a nap."

Delia needed a walk, in the direction of Whitaker's Inn. Now she had the excuse of seeing to rooms for Lady Presmacott when she awakened, and her maid and coachmen. The infant's cries had convinced Aunt Rosalie to remove there later, where all of Delia's arguments about crowded conditions at Faircroft House could not. Delia did not know whether it would be better for her aunt to confront the viscount at the inn, or his so-far undiscovered brother, here. She chose her own peace of mind and let Melinda cry for a minute.

"My stars, that brat's caterwauling is worse than Clarence's. A body could never get a moment's rest here, if the mattresses were not lumpy in the first place," Aunt Rosalie complained, before having her maid place a lavender-soaked cloth over her eyes. She was asleep and snoring in seconds.

Delia set out soon after. Before she had reached the high road, however, yet another coach pulled up Faircroft's drive, another large, crested coach. This time when the groom put down the stairs, a silver-haired gentleman of impressive height and nose stepped down, curling his lip at the plebeian surroundings. He did not speak, merely took out his quizzing glass to inspect the black-clad female who was standing in his way.

"Tell whomever is in charge here that he has callers, girl."

"I am in charge, my lord."

He looked her over again, head to toe and back up. "And who might you be, girl?" He addressed her as if Delia were an upper servant.

Delia curtsied. "I am Delia Croft, Lord Stivern." She had no doubt whatsoever as to the identity of this autocratic gentleman, even if he did not give her the courtesy of an introduction. The crest on the coach matched Lord Tyverne's signet, and the gentleman's brusque air of authority matched his son's commanding manner. She crossed her arms over her chest and raised her chin. "And this is my home." Into which she was not inviting this petty despot who had made such a mull of his progeny's lives, no matter how impolite she appeared. If the earl had been a more sympathetic parent, she believed, Ty would have taken his injured brother to the family seat, not to strangers.

"George Croft's sister?"

She had to lower her chin some to nod.

"Heard abut that. My condolences."

The way the earl's lip curled, Delia could not tell if he were expressing sympathy on her loss, or on her having a nodcock like George for a brother in the first place. "Thank you, my lord. I am afraid you have come too far on your journey, however. Your son is staying at the inn in the village. You might have passed him on the road."

"Tyverne? No, I checked at the inn. He hired a gig and left for London. I missed him by an hour. Fool coachman had us lost on some back road."

The look he gave the driver did not bode well for the man's continued employment. Delia gave him a look of commiseration and said "Oh, dear." Now she would have to wait until Ty returned with news of Thea's uncle before she could apologize. And now she had to face this large, imperious, eagle-beaked earl on her own. Oh, dear, indeed.

"If you head back to the City immediately, you might still catch up to him on the road, you know," she suggested.

"What, go back to Town and that parcel of mushrooms taking root in my town house? No."

"I believe those are my relatives, my lord."

"My condolences," he repeated. "I did not come to this godforsaken place to find Tyverne anyway."

"Oh, then whom did you seek?" She was not about to serve up poor Nonny on a platter to this monster. Thea would undoubtedly faint, and Nonny's recovery would be set back for weeks. Heaven only knew what Lord Stivern would do about their marriage. Since both parties were underage, she supposed he might be able to prevent it. "Ah, I know. You must have come to see your new granddaughter."

"My granddaughter, is it? Has anyone told you that you are impertinent, miss?"

"I believe your son has mentioned it."

"Humph. I shall be discussing the sudden addition to my family at another time. Right now I wish to see—"

"He is not here," Delia blurted, crossing her fingers at the lie.

"Ah, so the jackanapes is here. I wondered where he had gone to ground. You have been busy about my family's affairs, haven't you, Miss Croft?"

Delia ignored the personal slur. "Your youngest son was in a duel days ago, and you wondered? You did not come to find out his condition for yourself?"

The earl reached into his pocket and removed an elegant snuffbox. He raised a pinch of the stuff to his nose. "St. Ives lives, I assume?"

Delia nodded.

"Yes. Someone would have notified me else." The earl patted his nose with a lace-edged linen. "But I saw no reason to bestir myself over a schoolboy stunt, not when Tyverne had the matter well in hand. I did, however, come to find my daughter. She, at least, left word with her people as to her location."

Delia could not deny the duchess to the earl, could she? Goodness, she was swimming in deep water here. Luckily she did not have to lie this time. "Her Grace is on a tour of the cathedral at Canterbury with Mr. Stephen Anselm, a vicar there."

"Anselm, you say?" The earl stared at her, as if trying to decide where to start carving a cooked chicken. "How could such a little dab of a female have her fingers in so many pies, I wonder."

"I do not understand, my lord."

"No, I daresay you never knew the brazen puppy offered for my daughter when she was presented."

Ah, that explained a great deal, none of which Delia was going to discuss with the lady's father. "No, I thought they were good friends, nothing more."

"Then you are a fool, Miss Croft, which is the one thing I did not suppose you to be."

"Thank you, I think. At any rate, you will have a long wait for Her Grace. If you wish to repair to the inn"—not the parlor, inside—"I can tell her you called, or give her a message."

For a moment the earl looked unsure of himself. No, Delia decided, that had to be the light. He took another pinch of snuff, one-handedly, and said, "I came to tell her that her husband is gone."

"Gone to another house party? Gone to his Irish estates?" Delia knew all about Illington by now, and his mistresses.

"Gone to his Maker, by George. It gives a man pause when his friends start falling like flies. The duke was younger than I am, by Heaven."

The duke was an old satyr who had made his young wife miserable. This old ogre had nearly destroyed all four of his children's lives with his dictates and decrees. He had almost lost Ty altogether. Now Delia was supposed to feel sorry for him that he had lost a friend? "My condolences" was all she said.

Chapter 26

*I*f Major Lord Tyverne could ride into battle, Delia thought, she could be brave enough to face his father over tea. If that did not prove she was brave enough to be a soldier's wife, if that was what Ty wanted, then nothing would. So she invited the Earl of Stivern, surely the most assertive and self-assured man of her acquaintance, now that she realized Ty had feet of clay, or whatever, into her home. How could she not extend her hospitality when he was waiting for Ann with such news?

After sending Dover ahead with a warning, she led the earl up the narrow stairs. Nonny was established in one bedroom of the master suite, and Melinda's nursery was in the other, saving Nanny and the rest of them the additional climb up to the attic level.

Mr. St. Ives sat propped up on his pillows, wearing an old dressing gown of George's. Thea stood by his bedside, her hand in his. Delia could see the white knuckles of Nonny's hand, and the trembling in Thea's, but the girl did not faint, thank goodness. From her chaperoning seat by the window, Aunt Eliza slipped out the door after a brief introduction. "You know how I hate family confrontations, er, conversations," she whispered to Delia as she passed by.

The earl took out his quizzing glass and surveyed the pair in front of him. He noted his son's healthy color and steady gaze. "You'll do," he said with a nod of his silver-haired head. Then he fixed his blue-eyed scrutiny on Miss Dunsley. Thea's complexion turned ashen, as if she were the invalid, and her curtsy was a bit shaky, but she stayed upright, Delia was relieved to see.

"Miss . . . Dunsley, is it?" At Thea's nod, the earl continued: "If I were to offer you a sum of money to release my son from any cabbage-headed commitment he may have made, one, moreover, that is unenforceable by law, since he is a minor, would you take it and leave?"

Delia and Nonny both gasped at the man's audacity. Thea simply bobbed another curtsy, a steadier one this time, and said, "No, my lord. I would not leave unless Non—Mr. St. Ives wished me to go."

"Without first asking how big a sum I was willing to hand over?"

Thea shook her head. "No."

"Then you are as big a fool as my son, and you two deserve each other."

Nonny smiled and said, "I do mean to have her, Father."

The earl replaced his quizzing glass. "After dragging the family name through whatever muck Tyverne did not, I should hope so. And no havey-cavey Gretna nonsense, either, do you hear? There has been enough talk as is."

"No, sir. Ty is arranging a special license, for as soon as I am able to walk down the aisle."

"Good. And then you will bring your bride to Stivern Keep in Warwickshire. I am not getting any younger, you know. It is about time one of my sons knew something of the family lands. You'll train to be estate manager for that jackanapes brother of yours."

"I will?" There was nothing Nonny wished more, after marrying Thea. He could earn his own way, not accept charity from Ty. "That is, I will, sir! Thank you."

"Good. And see that you do not present me with any more premature grandchildren, ether, is that understood?"

Thea and Nonny both blushed, but they nodded.

"Fine." The earl turned to Delia then and said, "I suppose you are going to force me to view the infant next."

Delia had to smile. No one forced this man to do anything he did not wish. She led him back to the sitting room between the bedchambers and fetched Melinda out to him. Without asking, she put the sleeping child in his arms. Now the failing-sighted old fake did not have to use his peering glass to see the baby's perfect features.

"She is quite . . . lovely," the earl said. "My own were red-faced, squalling trolls, from what I recall. I am always amazed they turned out to be so handsome."

"Your family is indeed a good-looking one, from the three members that I have seen," Delia agreed, going to take the baby back.

"No, she is sleeping so peacefully, it would be a shame to disturb her. Melinda, you say? Pretty name. Pretty child. I would hold my first granddaughter a minute longer." He sat in the comfortable armchair, obviously prepared to sit longer than a mere moment—or toss thunderbolts at anyone daring to take the infant from him. "They are decent, too."

"My lord?"

"My sons and daughter. They turned out well."

Delia wanted to reply, "With no help from you," but she did not. Instead she said, "Excellently well. You should be proud," although she could not help the rude noise that escaped her lips.

"I take it you do not approve of me, Miss Croft."

"I am sure I would never be so presumptuous, my lord."

"Fustian. I think there is nothing you would not presume, not after seeing how you got this little lady so well established. In truth, you do not approve how I raised my children, do you, Miss Croft?"

"In truth? No. I would wish Melinda's father to be kind and caring, sharing her daily life, not be some distant godlike figure, sending orders down from his distant throne. I would wish her father to listen to her wishes, and help her make the right choices."

"I cared for my children. I did what I thought was best for them."

"Did you? Is that why you forced Ty into the army?"

"Force him? No one forces that boy to do anything. He was army mad from the day he could toddle. Horsey was his first word. He would have gone off to the cavalry when he turned six and ten. I tried to steer him in other directions, show him there were other ways of serving the country, get him leg-shackled so he could not run off. Bah. I should have saved my breath."

"And your second son, Aristotle?"

"Totty? The fool would have been content to manage my Irish stud, staying in Tyverne's shadow his entire life. Now he has a prosperous horse farm in Virginia. He is a wealthy landowner who might become governor, or senator, whatever they call the government there. My only regret is that he has children I might never see." He pulled the blanket closer around Melinda. "And Ann never had any."

"You married her to a man nearly your age."

"A rich man, who adored her. Frankly, I thought he would pop off years ago, leaving her a wealthy widow. What else was I to do, let her wed young Stephen Anselm, a cleric without connections or hope for advancement?"

"He has gone far, to the archbishop's own staff."

"With my son's help. But Anselm was a gazetted flirt then, with all the girls sighing over him. He would have broken her heart. Then she would have fallen prey to the next fortune hunter with a handsome face and a winning smile."

"He is still charming, but he never married."

"And she is finally a widow."

They both remained silent, contemplating the possibilities.

"What about Nonny, Mr. St. Ives, that is? I understand you wished him to become a cleric."

"What I wished was that the scapegrace learn to control his emotions and his impulses. Just look at this mare's nest he's made of finding a bride. No, I did not wish him to be a mere farmer, without education, without seeing something of the world so he did not miss it later."

"Yet you almost lost him."

"And Tyverne, too." The earl sighed. "Now that I am feeling Death looking over my shoulder, I wish I had done some things differently. A man does not want to be on the outs with his kin. Ann will make her own decision this time. She has enough wisdom to know when a man is after her money, and enough money to stay unmarried, if she wishes. Agamemnon will be happy to take his place at home and bring children and laughter to the old pile." He looked down. "This angel will be welcome there, to grow up with her cousins."

"Thea and Mr. St. Ives have already asked Lord Tyverne if they might keep her as their own. Ann, too, wishes to adopt her."

"Tyverne will do the right thing. He always does."

Delia nodded. "If nothing else, you did teach him all about duties and obligations." She could not put any enthusiasm in her voice, though. There was more to life than moral decisions.

"And honor. I taught him that," the earl said proudly.

"Yes, now if you had only taught him about love . . ."

The earl looked at her and the sleeping infant. "How could I instruct him about something I did not know? A woman who loves a man can teach him, though. I pray that is so."

So did Delia.

When Ann returned with Mr. Anselm to Delia's house, she was not visibly disturbed by the news of her husband's death. "The physicians told him his profligate ways would kill him. Now they have. I shall have to return to Illington's seat in Mansfield for the funeral, of course." Ann knew her duties and obligations, also.

Her father agreed. The duke's body was already being shipped there, on ice.

Ann would leave the next morning. "I will not be able to take Melinda with me, will I?" she asked, but answered herself. "No, of course not. Not for such a long journey, with her so tiny, and no wet nurse to travel with." A tear started to roll down her cheek. "And who knows how long I shall have to stay there? A house in mourning is no place for an infant."

No one gathered in that upstairs sitting room mentioned that this was also a house of mourning, chock-full as it was of aunts and an uncle ready to coddle the baby, to say nothing of a grandfather. The earl cleared his throat then. "I fear I cannot escort you, Ann. Before I left London, I heard rumors that Miss Dunsley's uncle had left town, vowing to get her back, and get his own back on St. Ives. I expect Tyverne to return as soon as he hears the same rumors, if not before, but with Agamemnon incapacitated, I cannot leave the women and infant undefended."

Thea clung to Nonny, and Delia made a note to have Mindle load his old blunderbuss. Ann said, "Of course not, Father. You are needed here. I shall have my maid and outriders to accompany me."

"Still," the earl pondered, "I cannot like leaving you without a man's protection, and not merely for the journey. Who knows what loose screws Illington's relatives might prove to be? You need a man's support, a trusted man to look after your interests until I can get there myself." He winked at Delia. "I wonder who . . . ?"

Ann's tears dried as if by magic as she put her hand in Reverend Anselm's waiting one. "I wonder, indeed, Father." She kissed the earl's lined cheek. "Thank you."

Then Aunt Rosalie woke up.

"What the devil are you running here, Dilly, a boardinghouse? People coming in and out, infants screeching, dogs yelping. Why, I hardly slept a wink, I swear, and you know how I need my afternoon nap. Not that I will do better at the inn, mind you, but if you will invite strangers to stay, instead of your own kin, I—" She noticed the earl. "Socrates? Socrates St. Ives? I should say Stivern, I suppose, although you had not succeeded to the title when I knew you."

The earl stepped forward and bowed. "Rosalie Croft! That is how I knew the name. I wondered, but did not have time to make inquiries. But you married that Presmacott chap, of course."

Aunt Rosalie waved her beringed hand in the air. "Gone this past decade. And your wife, Albertine?"

"Also departed."

"Really? I mean, it is really sad, is it not, to be on one's own in own's dotage?"

The earl, perforce, took the fingers Lady Presmacott held out to him and brought them to his lips. "You, in your dotage, Rosalie? Why, you are still as beautiful as that night we danced in the moonlight. Do you recall . . . ?"

Aunt Rosalie took the earl's arm and led him down the stairs. Then he turned back to glower at the giggles that followed him.

Ty was on his way back to Kent, his soldier's instincts telling him to hurry. Staying overnight with his man Winsted at an inn in London's seamier side had earned him two rewards: not having to face Sir Clarence, his wife, and Grim Gilbert, and information about Finster Dunsley. Thea's uncle, they learned, had recovered and subsequently fled from Town, along with his man-of-all-dirty-work, Ice Pick Porter.

Dunsley was being hounded by the duns and Sukey Johnson, all demanding money or his hide. One of his gambling partners had discovered a marked deck of cards at his house when they carried him there, unconscious after the duel, so the law was possibly looking for the knave, too, as were a few of his wagering victims. His niece was the only asset left to the man.

Thea was not safe.

Worse, Delia was not safe.

Worst of all, Ty learned when he sneaked through the kitchens of St. Ives House to raid the petty cash strong box, the Earl of Stivern was headed there, too.

Ty urged his pair faster.

Chapter 27

*T*y left his man Winsted off in the village, with instructions to get to Squire Gannon's place. The viscount wanted the guardianship of his brother's betrothed settled this very day. As soon as he turned his hired rig off the road onto the drive to Faircroft, he knew he was too late. A quick glance showed him Diablo out in the paddock next to the stables and an old cart with two horses hitched nearby. Closer to the house, one man held a screaming woman, the wet nurse, Ty recognized, Hester Wigmore. Even from this distance, Ty could see the glint of sunlight off a long, deadly blade held to her throat. That had to be Ice Pick Porter, the hired thug.

Another man held his pistol on a tall, silver-haired gentleman in a many-caped greatcoat. "Oh, hell," Ty swore, bringing his rig to a halt in a stand of trees, and leaping down. The man who held the gun aimed at Ty's father's chest had a curly-brimmed beaver perched atop white bandages on his head, like a snowman's hat. That had to be Finster Dunsley, soon to be a dead man. As Ty crept ahead, keeping to what cover the path offered, he saw Delia in her black gown come out the door, right into danger.

"Bloody hell."

Ty was well too far out of pistol range to chance a shot. He crouched and moved closer, trying to hide his bulk, in scarlet regimentals, no less, behind narrow trees and low shrubs. Luckily neither man was looking his way, for the tree trunks and ornamentals barely concealed a man of his size.

He made a quick dash to a thicker stand of bushes, almost within shooting range. That was all he saw before a solid object connected with the back of his head and darkness fell. No one had told him about Ice Pick Porter's brother, Brick.

Delia was upstairs with the earl when they heard the commotion. They had just seen the duchess and her vicar off, with her maid along to satisfy propriety, of course. The earl wished to see Melinda once more before heading back to the inn for breakfast with Lady Presmacott, which would be the first time in Delia's memory she'd ever heard of her aunt rising before noon.

Before Delia could go to the window to see what was making such a noise in the yard, Mindle came gasping up the stairs, his coat and spectacles all askew, the old blunderbuss in his shaking hands. "They've got Mrs. Wigmore, Miss Dilly. I'm afraid to shoot for hitting her." He had to sit down, wiping his brow.

Thea fainted and Aunt Eliza started wailing, but Delia had time for neither. She sent Dover to see if the back door was safe. If it was, he was to leave that way, to run for Jed in the stable, or for help in the village. Then she ran for the library, where George's pistol was stored, the one the army had shipped back to her. It was unloaded, of course, and she had no ammunition for it. The intruders might not know that, however.

By the time Delia got to the door, the earl had stepped out as if for a stroll in Hyde Park—right into the sights of a much larger gun. Delia had no doubts that that one was loaded.

Hessie Wigmore was still screaming, in the arms of a narrow-faced man with close-set eyes and a long, deadly knife at her throat. The earl was standing nonchalantly, one gloved hand in his greatcoat pocket. If this were a purple-backed novel, Delia knew, he'd have a pistol hidden there. In truth, she feared his lordship meant to pull out his quizzing glass. The man whose weapon was trained on the earl did not appear the type to appreciate such an affectation. Nor a touch of snuff, if the earl was about to offer it.

Of medium height, the armed man had dark stubble on his jaw and a thick bandage wrapped around his forehead, under a wide, curly-brimmed hat. An end of the white bandage was hanging loose, fluttering about his shoulders in the slight breeze.

"Put down your gun or I will shoot," Delia threatened in the strongest voice she could command, raising the pistol she held.

The man cocked his wrapped head to one side as if wondering if this slim, black-clad female would have the nerve to pull the trigger on a living target. "But you can't shoot both of us," he decided, "not with that pistol."

She could not shoot either, with an unloaded weapon, but Delia did not lower her gun.

"So either the nob or the woman dies, too," he said, spitting nearly at the earl's feet. "Now, I want my niece Thea," Dunsley continued more loudly, in case anyone had any doubt as to his identity, or anyone in the house had not heard him. "You get her out here now, and this swell and the screamer go free."

"I am afraid I do not know anyone of that name, sir," Delia said, stalling, but lowering the gun, since her bluff had failed and her arm was getting so tired she might drop the thing. "I am the only female here, other than the servants. You are wasting your time and breaking the law, I am certain. The magistrate has already been sent for."

"More reason to hurry," the man with the knife shouted.

"She's here all right," Dunsley yelled back. "This old cow told us."

"I'm sorry, Miss Dilly," Hessie Wigmore cried. "You never said as how I shouldn't mention the young lady. Only the young gentleman."

"So the bastard what stole my girl is here, too, eh? I

thought he might be, when I got wind where that brother of his went." Dunsley smiled, drawing attention to the white scar that hooked through one lip. "Better'n better. I'll want him out here, too. Might as well get my fun while I fetch the gel."

"Perhaps you would rather have a sum of money," the earl put in, wiggling his hand in the pocket, suggesting a purse.

"Oh, I'll never turn down a roll of soft, will I, Ice Pick?" Dunsley asked his confederate with a hoarse laugh. "But I still want the chit, and that blackguard what stole her, and did this"—he pointed to his head, where the bandage was coming more undone—"to me."

"No, I am sorry," Delia said before the earl could protest, or get himself killed with a reckless act of defiance, especially if he thought she could back him up with her empty pistol. Mindle and his blunderbuss would be no help, either, the way the old butler's hand was shaking. "But they have left for . . . for Gretna Green. Perhaps you saw a large traveling coach go by."

"'At's right, Fin, we did," the ruffian with the stiletto called over, growing anxious at the delay.

"And I looked in. Nobut a toff in spectacles and a female in furs, and a maid pretending they wasn't all over each other. Now quit your argle-bargle, missy, and get my niece out here. I've got a paying client waiting for her."

"That's reprehensible. You cannot send that child to a—"

"She's my kin and I can do what I want. Now send her out or I shoot this fine gent here."

White-faced, Thea started to go past Mindle, out the door toward Delia. "I will come, Uncle. Put your gun away and tell your man to release Mrs. Wigmore. She has done nothing to deserve your ill-treatment."

"No," Delia shouted, pulling her back and shoving her into Mindle's arms. "Your sacrifice will not save Nonny. Nor the earl, most likely. Dunsley has to keep him from following."

Dunsley laughed again, a chilling sound that brought goose bumps to the back of Delia's neck. "You're a downy one, missy, I'll give you that. Too bad we can't take you along, too. A spirited woman would bring a higher price. Some men like a female what puts up a good fight. And that red hair . . ."

Delia felt nauseated. And she could hear Nonny trying to make his way down the stairs on one leg.

"I'm going to count to ten. Then I am going to ruin your gentleman's fine coat here by blowing a hole through it," he told Delia, then said to the earl, "I'll try to miss that purse you offered, your lordship. One."

Help was not going to arrive in time.

"Two."

Delia knew in her heart that Dunsley would kill Ty's brother, and his father if the earl stood in his way.

"Three."

She glanced at the other man. He looked ready to stab Hessie Wigmore now, just to stop her caterwauling.

"Four."

Delia had only one option left; she whistled.

Ty returned to consciousness to feel agony in his skull and a heavy boot on his chest. He looked up to see a man even larger than he was, grinning down at him through missing teeth. The giant held a brick in his huge hand, daring Ty to make a move. He did not, waiting for a better moment for what he knew to be a futile attempt. He was outweighed, with a bad arm and the devil's own headache. And he was lying atop his pistol.

He could hear the conversation in front of the house, and despaired that he had failed them all. Nothing good could come of this and he'd been no help whatsoever. Worse, he'd brought Nonny and Thea into this trap, and brought the danger to Miss Croft's doorstep. Worst of all, the earl was there to see his son's inadequacy—and possibly die for it. He never wished to succeed the old curmudgeon, even less this way.

Then he heard an amazing sound. Delia had put her

fingers to her lips and let out an astounding, piercing whistle through that glorious gap in her teeth.

"What the . . . ?" the brick-wielding behemoth wondered, and so did Ty, and everyone else, seeing a little white dog come yipping toward them. Then they heard the thunder of hooves, and felt the ground shaking beneath them. Ty recalled some of George Croft's words, about getting the horse back: "Oh, I have only to whistle for him," the lieutenant had said, by Jupiter, and something about a circus.

Diablo cleared the paddock fence as if it were an enemy cannon he had to leap. Then he galloped across the lawn toward Delia, who screamed, "The hat, you spawn of Satan, go for the hat!"

Diablo charged. Angelina bounded. The horse headed for the wide-brimmed hat and the white cloth fluttering under it. The dog raced for her new owner, the one who always had treats in his pocket. She bit Brick on the ankle. Ty grabbed the man's other ankle while the lout was distracted and pulled him down, then rolled over and reached back for his own pistol. He bashed Brick over the head. Then he hit the big ox another time to make sure he stayed down, before running toward the house.

Ice Pick saw the dog and the soldier coming, and shoved Hessie Wigmore away from him, ready to throw the knife. The earl's shot stopped his arm before he could release the weapon.

Dunsley, meanwhile, was too busy running to think of shooting anyone. He lost his hat to those huge yellow teeth and hot breath. Then he lost his bandage, unwinding around him like a shroud. He lost part of his scalp, too, before he reached a tree. He might never have climbed a tree before in his life, but Finster Dunsley scrambled up that evergreen like a squirrel.

He would have shot the white horse, but his tree trunk was swaying, and then the gelding capered off, the bandage in his teeth a banner of triumph flying behind him.

In front of Dunsley, beneath his tree and out of range

of his pistol, was a half ring of armed men: the officer with his pistol, the earl casually but expertly reloading his prized Manton, the old butler with an equally as old weapon, young St. Ives with what looked like a fowling piece that might or might not be able to reach its mark across such a distance. Four fingers were quivering on four triggers, three aching to send this mawworm to Hell where he belonged; Mindle's because he was old.

Farther away, a groom stood guard, pitchfork in hand, and the Croft woman held a boy to her, his face turned into her skirts so he could not see.

Ice Pick was on the ground, cradling a shattered arm. Brick was out cold.

Dunsley could not win, but he could take one of them with him, whichever came within shooting range. "So which one of you brave hearts is going to step closer and fire, then?"

It was Squire Gannon, the magistrate, coming from behind with his rifle.

"There," Belinda's father said when the smoke cleared. "Now maybe I can sleep at night."

Chapter 28

The Porter brothers would be transported; Dunsley's body would be dumped. No one would miss any of them.

Nonny had been restored to his bed, his wound rebandaged. Thea, Aunt Eliza, and Mindle were resting, thanks to the laudanum drops, and a half a bottle of fine brandy the latter had unearthed. Hessie Wigmore had gone home, her milk curdled for certain.

Delia was upstairs, letting Squire Gannon offer Belinda's jewelry and a bottle of goat's milk to his baby granddaughter, once he had washed his hands, of course.

Lord Tyverne and his father were in the drawing room, sharing the rest of the brandy and a sigh of relief.

"Deuce take it, sir, I am sorry you got involved in this hobble," Ty began.

"Hell, I am sorry I did not shoot the dastard on sight. The rat-faced one might have run off, but I could not be sure, could I?"

"With gallow's bait like that? Never."

They both sipped their drinks, contemplating how different the outcome might have been, if not for Delia.

"Your Miss Croft is quite a woman, Tyverne."

"Amazing, isn't she?" the viscount agreed, possibly the first time in recent memory he and his father had concurred about anything. "I mean to have her, you know."

"You'd be a fool not to."

"I know you wished a higher-born woman to be countess eventually, and one with a larger dowry or property or connections."

"What father would not wish a wealthy bride for his son? Otherwise, I doubt I could find a finer wife for you, if I had to choose one myself." They both ignored the fact that the earl had been trying to do that very thing, almost since the heir's birth.

"Well, fortune or not, I mean to disappoint you again. If she will have me."

"Humph. I'd wager the woman is too canny to toss away a viscount, no matter what a mull you have made of your courting." The earl had spent a few moments with the estimable and informed Mindle, in addition to what he had gleaned from Lady Presmacott, and the evidence of his own eyesight, poor though it might be. "Furthermore, those were not my arms the chit threw herself into when the rowdydow was done. But what do you mean, disappoint me again?"

"Well, I certainly did not show to advantage this day. But I mean in my career. A dutiful son would have gone into the government, the way you wanted."

"Dutiful? Hah. If I had told you to become a soldier, you would have become a blacksmith. Nevertheless, you have made me proud, Tyverne. All the commendations and promotions, did you think I would not hear of them, not boast to my friends?"

Ty raised an eyebrow. "You might have written to me."

"What, and give you a swelled head? You had the generals to tell you what a good job you were doing."

The earl might have grown mellow with age, Ty reflected, and more compromising, with his compatriots keeling over. He had not grown more fatherly. Ty swirled the brandy in his glass, thinking how it no longer mattered. He would be a better parent, himself.

"She'd make a damn good wife for an officer," the earl said, after another pause to refill the glasses.

Mellow or not, the earl still wished his eldest son wed, it seemed. "She will not marry a soldier."

"No? Appeared to me as if she would follow you to the ends of the earth, but what do I know about women?"

"I would not ask her to follow the drum. That is no life for a lady. My arm is never going to be perfect, anyway, so I mean to sell out." Ty could not keep the bitterness from his voice. His life, his career—what was he to be, then? His father's son? An idle man about Town, waiting to be a richer one? Or else he could become a gentleman landowner, except he knew nothing of agriculture, and had no desire to learn. "I can work for the War Office, I suppose." Sitting at a desk seemed least appealing of all, but a man had to do something.

He must have imagined the earl's grunt of satisfaction, for Stivern said, "Tell me, how do you think the war is being fought?"

"Adequately, when the politicians let the generals in the field make the decisions. Why?"

"What about supplies? Munitions, uniforms, that type of thing."

"Hah. They are totally inadequate, when they arrive at all. And that is to say nothing of the pay owed the men who are fighting to keep the French from taking over the world, and England with it."

"And the treatment of injured soldiers when they are shipped home? The benefits paid to them, or the widows?"

"What benefits? And what is this about?"

The earl raised his glass. "You never did have an ounce of patience. Bear with me a moment. What do you feel about the plight of young women such as Miss Dunsley?"

"Being sold into prostitution? What man who calls himself a gentleman could consider it anything but an abomination?"

"And children younger than that boy Dover, working in the mines and factories all day, instead of going to school?"

"That is a sinful embarrassment to the country."

"Climbing boys? Transportation for stealing a muffin? Hanging for the most trivial of offenses? All of them, Tyverne. The injustices in this world go on and on. Now tell me, where do you think a man might have the best chance of making changes, making a difference?"

"In the government, of course," he had to admit, finally seeing his father's point.

"Of course." The earl drank down the last of his brandy and prepared to leave. Having missed breakfast with the lovely Rosalie, he was determined on lunch. "And Miss Croft would make an excellent wife for a cabinet minister or undersecretary."

Miss Croft, Ty considered after his father had left, would make an excellent wife for a prince or a pie man. If she would only say yes.

After the squire left, Delia could hear Ty coming up the stairs. No one else in the house moved so athletically. No one else in the house cursed with such vigor when he bumped his head on the low beam of the narrow stairwell. She started to smile until she remembered that the viscount had already been struck on the skull once this day. She rushed to the door, to find him standing there, rubbing his head.

Ty looked around and, seeing no one else present, not Nanny or one of the maids, and the door to Nonny's room closed, he would have backed out. He had no business ruining Delia's reputation, on top of all the other misfortunes he had brought her.

Delia had other ideas. She pulled him farther into the room, then threw her arms around him. He enfolded her in his own embrace, and to the devil with his weak arm and weaker principles. They clung together in relief that the Dunsley mess was over, in joy that they were all alive, in happiness that they were free to share such closeness, chest to chest, thigh to thigh, lips to lips.

Some time later, Delia remembered her terror. She

reached up to brush a lock of blond hair off Ty's fore-head. "I thought you were dead, when I saw you lying there!"

"My head is much too hard for that," he said, rubbing her back, stroking her neck below the crown of red braids. "But, Lud, when I saw you go out to confront that madman, I thought my heart would stop."

"I thought he would kill your father," Delia said, trembling in reaction, "and then come after Thea and your brother."

"He would have, if not for you. Thunderation, you saved all of their lives, my brave, brilliant, beautiful girl. And that is after saving mine from the fevers, and keeping Melinda from dying when her mother did. And taking in my brother, helping my sister reunite with Anselm, bringing my father here to see that his children are persons, not pawns."

"But I never had a hand in half of that, silly," Delia said from her secure place against Ty's chest, where she could hear his heartbeat if she listened very closely.

"None of it would have happened without you," Ty insisted. "I owe you such a debt of gratitude, it will take me a lifetime to repay. Will you let me try, my dearest Delia? Will you marry me?"

No matter how closely she listened, Delia was not going to hear the words she needed him to say. She stepped back, out of his arms, perhaps the longest step of her life. "No, my lord. I will not marry you while you speak of debts. I told you once and I will tell you again, I want no man who weds to fulfill his obligations, his sense of honor." She turned her back on him so he could not see the tears in her eyes. "Now go, unless you wish to help me change Melinda."

Ty went back to the inn. He did not get drunk, did not throw the water pitcher at Winsted when the man asked how things were at Faircroft House, and did not comment when his father announced that Lady Presma-cott had agreed to accompany him north for the funeral of Ann's husband. No, what he did was walk. He walked halfway to Canterbury, then turned around and walked halfway to Dover, it seemed.

How could the woman think that he wanted to wed her out of a sense of obligation? Hadn't she felt his desire in his kiss? Hell, hadn't she felt his arousal? And she had to know how he admired and respected her. He'd told her she was brilliant and brave, he knew, and there were no finer encomiums for a soldier to bestow. He was ready to give up his career, to raise her brother's child as his own instead of fostering the baby with his brother or sister. Didn't that prove his devotion? Thunderation, what more could the female want?

He should have taken the boy Dover along with him, or the plucky little dog. Either of them would have had better answers to Ty's questions.

The one thing he knew, with absolute conviction, was that Miss Delia Croft was meant to be his wife, and he was meant to be her husband.

Delia held the infant, Ty's baby, her baby. Although neither of them had actually given birth to Melinda, they had given her life. She had tried so hard not to grow fond of the child, to absolutely no avail. She might have tried to stop the sun from setting, more easily. So sweet and small, so helpless and soft—Delia thought her heart would break if she had to send Melly away, too.

Could a heart break twice? Hers was already shattered into jagged pieces that ached with every breath, every thought, every memory. Delia placed the infant back in the crib and wiped her eyes. How was she going to live without Ty?

And why the devil should she?

Chapter 29

*H*e was coming back. Delia knew he was. His brother was here, his daughter, his horse. Stalwart and steadfast, Ty was never one to turn his back on his duties. He would not turn craven and send messages, either, not this intrepid paradigm of valor. He had returned after she laughed at his proposal, hadn't he? He would come back. He had to.

Delia watched from the window, and had Dover keep a lookout while she went about her tasks. At last they spied the viscount walking up the drive, perhaps with less vigor than usual, but arriving soon, for all that.

Delia went out the back door, leaving a garbled message with Mindle that she was headed for the stables, seeing to some trouble to do with the horse. There might be any number of other equines in the Croft stables now, but when someone referred to the horse and trouble in the same breath, everyone knew which one. Usually they hid behind closed doors. Ty took off around the house at a run, despite the miles he had walked.

As usual, Jed Groom was not in sight, nor the other fellow Ty had never met. He could hear sounds from the end of the shadowed stable block, however, and headed there, to Diablo's stall. Then he heard the screams.

"Bloody hell!"

Delia was in the gelding's stall, pinned against the wall by the huge horse. Ty's stomach lurched. One flash of those iron-shod hooves, one lunge, one gnash of those powerful teeth—"Oh, God, no!"

He checked his pockets as he ran. No rum balls, no bonbons, not even a sugar cube. He did have his pistol, if it came to that. He hoped not. The horse had saved his life on the Peninsula, and perhaps his father's this very day. But Delia—

He began to talk, to call, to pray out loud, telling the horse to back away, telling Delia to edge along the side of the enclosure, closer to him. He could not shout the way he wanted, for who knew what the brute would do if further provoked. And his going into the stall might crowd the horse into rearing or slamming Delia against the walls.

Her face was white, and she seemed paralyzed by fear. He'd seen soldiers go immobile that way, unable to protect themselves, unable to run. Damn, he was going to have to bring her out. He opened the stall door and stood back, hoping Diablo would make a dash for freedom. No such luck. The horse was interested in Delia, only.

Ty edged into the stall, as far away from the gelding's rear hooves as he could get. "Come, Dilly," he called, "come to me. Come slowly, dearest, but come to me now." He held his hand out, begging her to try to move her feet.

She looked at him, her green eyes wide, and made a whimpering sound. Lud, he could not let anything happen to her. He kept his back to the wall and edged closer, crooning to her, to the horse, to anyone who would listen. "I'll come, sweetheart, don't worry, I'll come. I'll keep you safe this time, I swear. And she is not here to hurt you, my devil, no one is. I'll find you a hat or a bottle of ale, word of a St. Ives, just do not hurt her. There, come to me now."

He reached Delia's hand at last and, with a sudden pull, tugged her behind him, out of reach of those treacherous teeth. "Not safe yet, my love, but soon," he whispered to her. Diablo did not seem enraged, but one could never tell with the horse from hell. Ty could not carry Delia and protect her from the brute at the same time, but they had to get out of the stall. Or Diablo did.

Ty lunged. He raised his hands and charged, shouting as if in battle. "Get out, you worthless nag. Back. Get back, that's an order."

The white horse backed out of the stall, and Ty grabbed the door behind him, shutting them in, and the horse out. Let the brute go steal clothing off someone's wash line the way he did in Spain, or trample the ornamentals, as he did in London. Hell, let him go take a piece out of that worthless groom who was never around when one needed him. "I don't care if you never come back!" Ty called after him, before he turned around and caught Delia up in his arms, vowing he would never let her go again.

Delia had to tug at his collar before her ribs were crushed.

"Oh, Lord," he said, loosening his grip by about a quarter of an inch. "I have never been so frightened in my life, Dilly. Just let me hold you awhile, please."

So she did. And enjoyed the feel of his strong arms around her, and the smell of him, all soap and horse and man. After a minute, she raised her head and said, "You saved my life, you know."

Ty was too busy savoring the feel of her to think straight. She was alive, and that was all that mattered. "I suppose so. Your brother told me to save someone else."

"That means we are even, Ty. I saved you, you saved me. No more debts."

"No more . . . ?" He smiled. "You are right. The tally is tied. No more pluses and minuses." Then he grinned more broadly. "If I saved your life, does that mean I get to keep you? To look after for forever, the way Dover says it works?"

"If you still want."

"Lud, I want nothing more. But you said you would never marry a soldier, so first I will—"

"You can stay a soldier forever, my dear, as long as I

can come along. I would follow the drum with you, rather than ask you to give up what you are."

"No, a soldier is not who I am, it was what I did. I can still serve my country with honor, just in other ways. So will you marry me, Miss Delia Croft? I will not get down on my knee again, certainly not inside a horse's stall."

Delia smiled back. "Say it, Ty. Say it first."

"Say it . . . ?"

"The words, you great gossoon. Say the words. I swear your tongue will not fall out and the roof will not fall in on us."

"You mean I love you? That's what you've been waiting for? But I must have loved you from the instant I fell at your feet. You have not been out of my thoughts or my dreams since, no, not even during my wedding to Belinda. How could you not know that?"

"Oh, Ty, I have loved you for so long, it seems, waiting for you to know your own heart."

"More like ready to know I had one, I suppose." He placed his hand between them, over his heart. "I still have none, my dearest Dilly. It belongs to you."

"Dilly? You do not think I am Delia anymore?"

"Oh, she is much too elegant and refined for a battered old soldier." He removed a wisp of straw from her hair. "And she would never kiss me in a stable."

Kiss him she did, with all of her love and dreams and hopes and happiness.

"I take it that is a yes?" Ty asked sometime later.

"Yes, my lord, I would be honored to marry you, to share your name and your daughter and your future, wherever it leads us."

"Truly you have made me the happiest of men, darling. It would be miracle enough that you love me. Better yet, I shall never have to go through a wretched proposal again. Best of all, I'll have you by my side for the rest of my life."

Which, of course, required another kiss to seal their pledge.

The horse got tired of waiting for his reward. He stuck his head over the stall door and snorted.

Ty looked over at those big brown eyes, then down into Delia's green ones. "You never told me, my love. What possessed you to go into Diablo's stall?"

"Why, so you could save me, of course!"

"But you could have been killed, you fool! Everyone knows he hates men."

Delia reached over and stroked the horse's velvety nose. "But he loves women. Especially the one who rescued him from that traveling circus."

Signet Regency Romances
from

ELISABETH FAIRCHILD

"An outstanding talent." —*Romantic Times*

CAPTAIN CUPID CALLS THE SHOTS
0-451-20198-1

Captain Alexander Shelbourne was known as Cupid to his
friends for his uncanny marksmanship in battle. But upon
meeting Miss Penny Foster, he soon knew how it felt to
be struck by his namesake's arrow....

SUGARPLUM SURPRISES
0-451-20421-2

Lovely Jane Nichol-who spends her days disguised as a
middle-aged seamstress-has crossed paths with a duke who
shelters a secret as great as her own. But as Christmas
approaches-and vicious rumors surface-they begin to wonder
if they can have their cake and eat it, too...

To order call: 1-800-788-6262